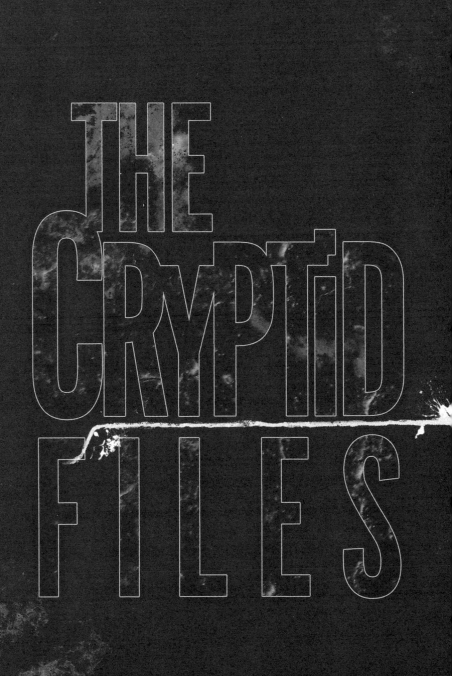

#3 THE PACIFIC

GIANTS

JEAN FLITCROFT

MINNEAPOLIS

First American Edition published in 2014 by Darby Creek, an imprint of
Lerner Publishing Group, Inc.

Copyright © 2012 by Jean Flitcroft

First published in Dublin, Ireland in 2012 by Little Island as The Cryptid
Files: *Pacific Giants* by Jean Flitcroft

Darby Creek
A division of Lerner Publishing Group, Inc.
241 First Avenue North
Minneapolis, MN 55401 USA

For reading levels and more information, look up this title at
www.lernerbooks.com.

Front cover: © Dale O'Dell/Alamy.

Main body text set in Janson Text LT Std 12/17.
Typeface provided by Linotype AG.

Library of Congress Cataloging-in-Publication Data

Flitcroft, Jean.
    The Pacific giants / by Jean Flitcroft.
        pages   cm. — (The cryptid files ; #3)
    Summary: "Vanessa discovers another beast, cadborosaurus willsi, or
Caddy for short, off the west coast of Canada"— Provided by publisher.
    ISBN 978–1–4677–3266–6 (lib. bdg. : alk. paper)
    ISBN 978–1–4677–3486–8 (eBook)
    [1. Sea monsters—Fiction. 2. Canada—Fiction. 3. Horror stories.]
I. Title.
PZ7.F65785Pac 2014
[Fic]—dc23   2013024086

Manufactured in the United States of America
1 – SB – 12/31/13

For Mers and Als

CRYPT*O*ZOOLOGY

Cryptozoology is the study of strange creatures that some people believe they have seen but for which there is no scientific proof. These creatures are called cryptids. It comes from the Greek word *kryptos*, meaning hidden. Those who study these animals are called cryptozoologists.

The first book in the Cryptid Files series, *The Loch Ness Monster*, is about the most famous cryptid. The second, *The Chupacabra*, features a creature that drains the blood of other animals and whose Spanish name means "goatsucker."

This book is an adventure set off the west coast of Canada, where Vanessa comes face-to-face with an extraordinary sea creature. This huge beast is part of local mythology but has been seen by so many people that it has been given a scientific name, *Cadborosaurus willsi*.

PROLOGUE

The creature rose out of the water just in front of her, as though commanded by her thoughts. Vanessa froze, too terrified to swim. She clutched the red-and-white lifesaving ring, and prayed feverishly that the beast wouldn't notice her.

But the large, ugly head pivoted on its long neck. Its eyes bulged; its jaw dropped open; and then the snakelike coils appeared—huge, heavy, and powerful.

Oh, God! Please help me, Mum, Vanessa pleaded silently. *Make it go away.*

She watched it sink slowly down into the water again. But that didn't help. It was bad enough seeing a sea serpent above the water, but how much worse to imagine it swimming beneath her at that very moment!

Vanessa felt a current of water rush past her legs and saw it well up around her in a smooth, circular pattern. She gave a strangled cry, let go of the ring, and swam for her life. The cold had crept into her bones and her teeth rattled in her head like boiled sweets in a jar. With each stroke she got a little weaker.

The beach wasn't all that far. Surely she could make it.

CHAPTER 1

On 5 October 1933, the *Victoria Daily Times* was the first newspaper to publish a story about a "real" sea monster that lived in the Gulf of Georgia, British Columbia, Canada. The sightings were made by two witnesses, a lawyer and an official at the Provincial Library of Victoria, who saw it independently and on different dates and were considered above suspicion.

Vanessa leaned against the rail of the ferry and stared out across the expanse of gray sea. Her eyes watered in the wind and her hair whipped across her face, making it difficult to see anything. Vancouver seemed a long way behind her now, and the gulf stretched like a huge empty canvas before her. Land was just about visible on the horizon, but the thin layer of mist that had descended made it hard to guess the distance to Duquette Island.

In front of her, the seagulls circled and skimmed the choppy water thrown up by the engines. Their hoarse shrieks of delight punctuated the monotonous thud of the engines pounding away beneath Vanessa's feet.

What freedom birds have! she thought. *And what fun to fly like that!* Vanessa looked around. As there was nobody else on the deck, she stretched out her arms, face to the wind, and imagined the feel of the wind under her wings, the moisture of the clouds on her face.

The ferry lurched suddenly. Before Vanessa had time to grab hold of the rail, she was thrown backward along the deck and fell heavily at the feet of an elderly man. Flustered, she jumped up and started to apologize, but the wind carried her words away and the man continued to ignore her. He stared silently out to sea, looking so frail and white that Vanessa wondered how he had managed to stay on his feet—he wasn't even holding on to anything.

Where had he appeared from? She hadn't seen him in the lounge earlier or on deck when she came out. He was probably a local. His yellow raincoat suggested that he was better prepared for the unpredictable weather in Canada than a tourist like her. Maybe he was feeling seasick and just wanted to be left alone.

Vanessa turned away and walked purposefully toward the stairs which led inside. It was time to join Lee—her father's girlfriend, and now also a good friend of Vanessa's—in the warm lounge. It would be much easier to ignore the stale smell of sick in there now that she was freezing cold. Her thin cotton jacket was drenched through. So much for the start of summer in Canada and the clear blue skies she had imagined! Gloves and a woolly hat would have been a lot more useful.

Lee was sitting exactly as Vanessa had left her, with a cup of coffee in one hand and a book in the other, her glasses perched on the bridge of her nose. Vanessa threw herself down on the chair beside her, and Lee looked up, surprised.

"You're soaked, Vanessa. I didn't realize it was

raining." Lee dropped her book onto her knee and looked out the window.

"It's not rain as such, just very wet mist," Vanessa replied, pushing the wet strands back off her face. "An attractive look, huh?"

"Have some coffee. It'll warm you up."

Lee offered Vanessa her cup and Vanessa took a slug.

"Blah," she said, shaking her head and making a face. "It's lukewarm."

Vanessa leaned her head back and closed her eyes. The chairs were uncomfortable and she was restless.

"Lee, have you ever wondered why it's called lukewarm?" Vanessa said suddenly. "Could it ever have been johnny-warm or henry-warm, do you think?"

Lee grinned at Vanessa.

"You're bored, my dear. The rubbish you talk gets much worse when you're bored, I've noticed."

"True," Vanessa replied solemnly. "So you can imagine how bad I am at school."

Vanessa stretched out across a couple of seats and took out the travel guide that she had bought in Vancouver. She had tried to read it earlier, but the combination of the smell in the lounge and the hard plastic seats, which gave her dead legs, had forced her out onto the windy deck.

"It's not boredom really, Lee. I'm just impatient to get to Duquette Island. I'm dying to see what it's like."

"Well, it's just another forty minutes or so," Lee said, checking her watch. It was half past five. "Mrs. Bouche from the guesthouse says she'll be at the ferry terminal to pick us up."

Vanessa looked around the lounge. Most people had gotten off at the last stop—Galiano Island. Apart from herself and Lee, there were now just four women and two men left in the lounge—making seven passengers total, if you included the grumpy man on deck. Only two of them were chatting; the others sat silently reading or preoccupied by their thoughts. Were these people visiting Duquette Island, like herself and Lee, or did they live there? If so, they might know Mrs. Bouche, the guesthouse owner. One of them might even be a relation.

"Maybe the guy in the raincoat is Mrs. Bouche's husband," Vanessa wondered out loud. "No, her father, more like it."

"What guy?" Lee looked puzzled.

"Oh, a man I almost knocked down when I was up on deck. He was wearing this bright yellow raincoat and just appeared out of nowhere." Vanessa frowned. "He didn't seem all there, actually—very tired and ill-looking."

"And what's he got to do with Mrs. Bouche?"

"Nothing, probably," Vanessa admitted.

Lee opened her book again and started to read. Vanessa flicked through the pages of her guidebook.

"Oh, look, here we are—page 192. Listen, Lee." Vanessa cleared her throat theatrically.

"'Duquette Island is one of the remote Gulf Islands off Vancouver in Canada, with a permanent population of just 327 people. A traveler will be struck by the curly arbutus trees adorning the moss-covered rocky slopes that run down to the ocean's edge. The island is fanned by a steady breeze and has an intoxicating scent—the rarest of finds these days: the heavenly perfume of pure, fresh air.'"

Vanessa stopped reading. "Wow," she said sarcastically, turning some more pages.

"Go on," Lee said. "It sounds nice." Vanessa raised her eyebrows and grinned.

"No, that's it, Lee! That's all they say about

Duquette. Imagine—fresh air is the highlight."

A small frown settled on Lee's forehead.

"Well, don't say I didn't warn you, Vanessa," she said. "This was never meant to be a holiday. I'm here to work and you're here to . . . to . . ." Lee stuttered to a halt.

"Tag along?" Vanessa offered mildly.

"You knew it was a remote island and that you'd have long hours on your own in a guesthouse. You said you didn't mind. Remember?" A hint of panic colored Lee's voice.

"Oh, I'm only messing, Lee. You know me: resourceful, self-contained," Vanessa replied mischievously. "I'll just enjoy the intoxicating perfume and the curly trees, and you can work away on your whale stuff. You'll hardly notice I'm there. I promise."

Lee turned away to smile. Vanessa was a thirteen-year-old who was hard not to notice. Her beautiful face and slim figure caused heads to turn, although Vanessa seemed oblivious to it. It was her uncanny ability to get herself into "difficult situations" that was the real problem with Vanessa.

CHAPTER 2

An ocean without its unnamed monsters would be like a completely dreamless sleep.

—The Log from the Sea of Cortez, *John Steinbeck*

The rest of the journey passed slowly. Lee read her book while Vanessa shifted restlessly on her chair and eventually went outside on deck again.

"Just going to check if that man is still upright," she whispered in Lee's ear as she went out.

Vanessa returned about five minutes later and

shook her head.

"Gone. And the weather's getting worse. Definitely a bit of a storm brewing."

Lee looked at her watch again. Although it had only been two hours, this bit on the boat had felt like the longest leg of the journey from Dublin. Vanessa's prowling definitely hadn't helped.

"Ten more minutes, I'd guess," Lee said.

"Lee," Vanessa said suddenly, "I know you work for Greenpeace. But why are you here? All you've told me is that it's something to do with whales."

"Okay, well, you know that Greenpeace's main aims are to help conserve the planet and to protect endangered species."

"Like whales," Vanessa added.

"Yes. There's now a worldwide ban on commercial whaling, and that's helping to bring up the numbers of whales. But this is an important area for whales, and there's a research center here on Brighton Island that I'm going to visit."

Lee smiled at Vanessa and opened her book as if she were about to start reading.

Vanessa was puzzled. Lee hadn't really answered her question.

"Yes, but why are you here? Is there a problem?" Vanessa persisted.

Lee held Vanessa's gaze and wondered how much she should tell her. She wasn't used to discussing her work with young people, but there was no way Vanessa was going to be fobbed off.

She sighed. "Well, Dr. Mitchell's research involves tagging some of the killer whales and humpbacks in this area so they can track them by GPS and observe their migration patterns and behavior."

"And . . . ?"

"Apparently, quite a few of their tagged humpbacks have gone missing recently."

"Gone missing?"

"Well, the scientists have lost the GPS signal for them, so they don't know where the whales are. They think that's suspicious."

"Can't a tag just fall off by accident?" Vanessa leaned forward, interested.

"Of course. Occasionally it happens because it's not attached properly in the first place or it's rejected by the whale's body. But not in such large numbers."

"Why don't they go to the police?" Vanessa asked innocently.

Lee laughed. "A few tons of blubber going missing in the ocean is the least of their problems in Vancouver, I'm afraid."

"So that's why they asked Greenpeace in? Cooool!" Vanessa's eyes shone with excitement. "Maybe Duquette Island's going to be a really sinister place after all." She made a mock ghostly sort of sound: "Wooo!"

"Not sure Duquette sees much action," Lee said with a chuckle. "Unlikely to be much mystery with a population of 327 and thousands of curly-something trees."

Vanessa sighed. "True."

"Maybe I'll be able to bring you to the research laboratory on Brighton Island on one of the days," Lee said kindly.

Vanessa's face lit up. She threw a punch in the air and jumped to her feet.

"I'm just going back out to see how close we are now."

A wave of affection washed over Lee. It had been a rocky start when she had first started going out with Vanessa's father two years ago, but they were great friends now.

CHAPTER 3

A sea serpent has been part of the local Indian folklore and legends on the Gulf islands off Vancouver for many hundreds of years. The white settlers who came to those parts in the early 1900s called it the "Sea Hag" because of the fear it inspired.

Their welcome to the island by Mrs. Bouche was a windswept and flustered one. It was clear by now that a major storm was brewing. The boats in the harbor bobbed about and clanked like warning bells.

Vanessa looked around to see if the guy in the

raincoat was getting off, but there was no sign of him. Perhaps he had been one of the crew all along. If so, she guessed he wouldn't have many journeys left in him. He had looked too frail to work at all.

Mrs. Bouche was a big woman who wore an enormous overcoat and clumpy hiking boots, and it was with some difficulty that they made their way up the hill from the harbor to her car. Despite the fact that Lee and Vanessa had their backpacks, Mrs. Bouche was struggling for breath by the top.

"In the car, in the car," she panted at them, indicating the smallest, most battered car Vanessa had ever seen in her life.

When she opened the boot, it was full of gardening equipment and tools, and there was no room for their luggage. Inside, much of the backseat was taken up with plastic bags.

"Sorry about that; stuff for the parish fair in a couple of weeks. You'll have to put your bags on your knees," Mrs. Bouche shouted over the noise of the wind. "I asked Wayne to empty the car earlier, but he must have forgotten."

It didn't take long for it to become evident that changing gears with Lee's bag in the front was too awkward for Mrs. Bouche. So, after a lot of reorganization, both backpacks were jammed into the backseat with Vanessa sandwiched between them, the plastic bags under her feet.

"It's no distance, honey," Mrs. Bouche said cheerfully over her shoulder to Vanessa.

As the car pulled away, the heavens opened and the rain fell—although they were more like water bombs than raindrops. The windscreen wipers had only one speed, and unless Mrs. Bouche had an all-seeing eye, Vanessa thought, she couldn't possibly see the road ahead. However, jolly Mrs. Bouche was unfazed and managed to keep up a stream of happy chatter as she drove—high and low tides, walks in Fulham Woods, the Reverend Took's parish fair, and Wayne's addiction to Jo-Jo's.

Between the noise of the rain and the bags surrounding her, Vanessa could hear only snatches of the conversation up front and could see nothing at all of the scenery. Relaxing back into her seat, she let her thoughts drift. She was more resourceful than most teenagers, but could she really survive a week here on her own for most of each day? Maybe convincing Lee to bring her along had not been her best idea.

It was only ten minutes by her watch, but it seemed ages to Vanessa, before they pulled into the driveway of the guesthouse. The huge trees in the front garden swayed violently, and she could hear them creaking and moaning. *Are these the famous arbutus trees?* she wondered. But it was not the time to start that conversation.

Mrs. Bouche pulled the car up so close to the front door that if she'd gone any farther they would have been in the hall.

"Welcome to Rocky Bay," she announced grandly. "Just make a dash for it and put your stuff into the first room on the right."

Vanessa smiled to herself. This Mrs. Bouche was quite a character—and she seemed nice too.

Lee and Vanessa struggled with the car doors catching in the wind as they got out. They hurled themselves through the front door and then found the first room on the right, as they had been told. It turned out to be a pleasant little sitting room with the biggest TV screen that they had ever seen. An *X-Factor* performer was singing his heart out, rolling his eyes and clutching his heart to indicate the pain of heartbreak, but there was no one watching.

"I'm sure Wayne's around somewhere," Mrs. Bouche said, coming into the room behind them. "I left him right there on the couch. He wanted to show you to your rooms and help with your bags," she said fussily, patting her damp hair back into place.

Wayne did not appear, so Vanessa and Lee trailed after Mrs. Bouche's wheezing form as she climbed the stairs to their bedrooms. Luckily they were right next door to each other. Mrs. Bouche suggested that they come down for something to eat, but neither Lee nor Vanessa had any appetite for food or for the conversation they would have to make. They both felt exhausted after the long journey. A shower and a bed were all either of them could think of.

CHAPTER 4

In 1933, a lawyer and his wife from Victoria who saw a sea creature while on their yacht described it as a "horrible serpent with the head of a camel."

When Vanessa woke the next morning and looked out of her window, she felt as if a weight had been lifted from her shoulders. It was so beautiful. The sea was a dark blue and the sky was clear. Her bedroom was really very pretty too.

Vanessa knocked gently on the wall of Lee's

bedroom, but there was no reply. Maybe Lee was still asleep. Perfect: that meant that there was no rush for her to get up.

She opened her window and felt the cool air pour in. Duquette Island fresh air—the guidebook was right: There was nothing quite like it! When she leaned out, she could see a long stony beach stretching out below. She wondered where the steps down to it were.

A sound on the stairs and muffled conversation made Vanessa start slightly. She had forgotten that there might be other people staying in the guesthouse. It was hard to imagine any casual tourists turning up on Duquette Island, though—it was well and truly off the beaten track. She heard a door clunk farther down the landing and some footsteps on the stairs. Then all went quiet.

By the time Vanessa had showered and dressed, she was ravenously hungry. She knocked a couple of times on Lee's door on her way downstairs, but there was no answer.

The guesthouse was bigger than Vanessa had imagined on arrival, and she took a few wrong turns before she finally found the kitchen at the back of the house. There was nobody there, and she could see that the kitchen table was set for only one person.

Vanessa stood for a moment, unsure what to do. She had turned to go back up and find Lee when Mrs. Bouche's cheerful voice boomed out from the pantry.

"Welcome, welcome. Cayde mil foilte." Mrs. Bouche mangled the Irish greeting but grinned with pride at the achievement. "Lee taught me how to say welcome in your language, but it took a bit of practice to get it good."

Vanessa laughed. Mrs. Bouche was infectious in her enthusiasm. "Don't I know it! I've been doing it since I was five and I'm not much better."

Mrs. Bouche looked a bit deflated, so Vanessa hurried on: "I mean, your *céad míle fáilte* was really good. It's just a very hard language to learn."

"Anyway, sit down, sit down. Normally people from Europe wake early when they visit here. Jetlag makes them wake really early," she babbled on, "but you're late and not early. Hungry, honey? I'm sure you're hungry. Everyone is always hungry here—it's the fresh air, you know."

Vanessa smiled up at her. That famous fresh air again.

"Now, you just tell me what you'd like for breakfast." Vanessa's mind drew a blank for a moment.

"Uh, toast?" she said finally.

"That it?" Mrs. Bouche didn't try to hide her disappointment.

"Actually, I'll just have whatever Lee is having. She'll be down shortly."

"Ah, bless you, honey. Dr. McDonald went about her business hours ago. She was up at the crack of dawn and said she'd be home around three o'clock today so you'd have some of the afternoon together."

Mrs. Bouche prattled on about Lee's breakfast and what she had eaten, oblivious to the stricken look on Vanessa's face.

Vanessa knew that Lee was here to work, but she hadn't expected her to disappear without saying a word on their first day. In her own head she had even hoped that she could go with her to the research laboratory on Brighton Island today.

"So it's pancakes you want," Mrs. Bouche finished up, getting out a large frying pan and slapping it down on the range. "Plenty of plump pancakes prepared perfectly," she said playfully. "Coming right on up," she added with an exaggerated drawl.

Oh, dear, Vanessa thought. Hopefully this whole experience wasn't going to be too painful. How on earth was she going to spend her days in Rocky Bay Guesthouse alone with Mrs. Bouche?

The breakfast was amazing, though, and by the time Vanessa had polished off two pancakes smothered in fresh blueberries and almost a whole jug of maple syrup, she felt a lot better. She came to the conclusion that she'd have to get used to pottering on her own from day one.

Vanessa refused seconds politely. It was time to explore the place.

"What's the best way to get down to the beach, Mrs. Bouche?" she asked as she carried her plate to the sink.

"Oh, please call me Frankie. Everyone else does—even Wayne does sometimes."

Who exactly was this Wayne that she kept talking about? Vanessa wondered. It was clear that Frankie thought she should know.

"Do you mind me asking who Wayne is?" Vanessa asked, recalling something about his addiction to Jo-Jo's, whatever that was.

Mrs. Bouche burst out laughing, as if Vanessa had

said the funniest thing in the world, although she also looked mildly incredulous.

"Why, honey, Wayne is my son, of course." Her laugh turned to a fond chuckle. "Wayne is my one and only."

Mrs. Bouche said her son's name with such naked affection and reverence that Vanessa was quite taken aback.

Vanessa's dad didn't talk about her brothers like that, and he certainly had never used *her* name with such open admiration. She'd have to talk to him about that when she got home!

"What age is Wayne?" Vanessa asked, not sure what she was hoping for. Too young could be annoying; her own age could be complicated.

"He's ten, but he's big for his age," Wayne's mother said with pride. "He's been so excited about you coming, honey. He's just dying to show you the ropes. He had his breakfast earlier and went off on his bike, but he'll be back soon, I'm sure."

CHAPTER 5

We don't know all the sea creatures in our world yet. Marine scientists believe that there are many large deepwater species yet to be discovered. In 2005 two scientists, Solow and Smith, predicted that as many as fifteen marine mammal species still await discovery.

Vanessa put her camera, iPod, and sketchbook in her backpack and made her way to the garden. To the side of the house, she found a small rusty gate that was half off its hinges. She stepped over it and followed the path around to the back of the house. At the end of that was another gate. This one was held open with an old piece of string. Below it she could see tiled steps disappearing down, many of them broken. Clearly nothing around here had been repaired for a long time.

Vanessa started cautiously down the steps. At one point there was an entire step missing, and there was a long and dangerous drop to the beach. Vanessa shuddered. She wasn't bad with heights, but the jagged rocks below looked a bit scary. Had other guests not mentioned the state of the steps to Frankie? Did they get many guests?

Vanessa looked around. It was a very beautiful spot, but what a lonely life for Mrs. Bouche and Wayne! *What must it be like in winter?* she wondered.

Vanessa walked the full length of the beach before deciding to take off her runners to have a paddle. The sea, which had looked quite blue from her bedroom window, now looked gray and very cold. *A bit like the sea at home in the summer*, Vanessa thought. She'd have to test it.

She sat down on a boulder and began to peel off her socks. Suddenly there was a scrabbling noise behind her and Vanessa turned quickly, expecting to see a dog or a small animal, but there was nothing there. It happened again, the sound a little closer this time, so she sprang up to investigate. Through a crevice in one of the rocks an enormous crab, with the longest legs she had ever seen, scuttled toward her quickly. Startled, Vanessa stumbled backward and landed hard on the flat of her back.

"Ouuuuch," she shouted into the air, when she finally recovered her breath. It had been a painful fall.

The noise she heard next sounded exactly like a snicker. A small, unpleasant, half choked-back snicker, Vanessa could have sworn. She sat up quickly, wincing with the pain, and looked around. Who could it be? She hadn't seen anyone on the beach.

And then it struck her.

"Come on out, Wayne," she said as playfully as she could.

"I know you're there!" She hoped the irritation in her voice wasn't too obvious.

Vanessa waited.

"Come on, Wayne. It's OK. Your mum said you would follow me down to the beach."

Her voice was friendlier this time. It would be better to take a more conciliatory approach, she thought.

After all, Wayne was only ten—and she would be seeing him every day for the next week.

The silence was total, except for the soft sound of the waves and the birds calling out overhead. She made a complete circle of the area, checking behind boulders. Nothing. Maybe she had been imagining things.

Vanessa rubbed her shoulder, which had taken the brunt of her fall. It was pretty sore, but she didn't feel like going back to the guesthouse yet. Time for a paddle. Slowly rolling up the legs of her jeans, Vanessa listened hard, but there were no more snickers or scuttling sounds.

At the water's edge, a wave ran over her feet and made her gasp. It was just as cold as the Irish Sea—or just as "refreshing," as her mum used to say on their caravan holidays in Wexford when Vanessa was younger. She smiled to herself, remembering the bets as to who would be in first. It had always been Vanessa. Her brothers, Luke and Ronan, liked to talk tough, but they were wimps when it came to it.

The sound of a bell ringing above her made Vanessa turn and look up. From the beach side, the guesthouse looked a rather odd building—sort of straggly, as if it had evolved over time. Some of the rooms looked as if they were balancing uncomfortably on the edge—one-buttock-on-a-shared-seat sort of uncomfortable. A decent storm could easily blow it down the cliff, Vanessa thought.

The bell tinkled again. A clear, sweet sound like the little handbell her headmistress rang in school to bring order. "A lady never raises her voice," she reminded them frequently.

But what did the bell mean here? A lunch bell? Surely not. She'd only just eaten breakfast.

Vanessa looked at her wrist, but she'd forgotten to put her watch back on after her shower. She had no idea how long she'd spent on the beach, and as it had clouded over, she couldn't even use the sun to help her guess. She paddled for a bit longer and then dried her feet on her jeans. She put on her runners, but shoved her socks into her pocket, and made her way slowly up to the guesthouse, stopping to look for the giant crab that had startled her earlier. If she found it, she'd take a photo to show to Lee later. But the crab was well gone.

When Vanessa finally poked her head around the door of the kitchen, Mrs. Bouche was sitting with a young boy at the kitchen table, eating.

"Don't you worry about being late, honey," Frankie said as she got up to get a plate for Vanessa. "Your first day here gives you the perfect excuse, doesn't it, Wayne?"

The boy stared glassy-eyed at Vanessa.

"It's the perfect excuse, isn't it, Wayne?" Frankie repeated. She didn't seem in the least put out when he didn't reply. Maybe he couldn't speak? That would be perfect: pleasant, smiling interactions with no expectation of conversation or friendship. Surely Frankie would have said something to her earlier, though.

"Hi, Wayne," Vanessa said politely, pulling out a chair opposite him.

Wayne stopped eating and winked at her. Vanessa's eyes widened. Had he really just winked at her? She stared at him, her jaw loose with surprise, and watched a slow grin spread across his face like a rash.

There was something unpleasant about him, and Vanessa took an instant dislike to his face. Not his features so much as his look. Smugness? Sneakiness? Was that even a word? She shook herself mentally. Maybe it was just the thought of him spying on her at the beach that was coloring her first impression.

"Been to the beach yet?" Wayne asked her

suddenly. "If not, I'll take you later if you like."

Frankie beamed.

"See, I told you my Wayne was dying to show you the ropes, Vanessa. He knows all the best walks and hikes on the island."

Vanessa eyed Wayne warily. His eyes slid away from hers. Sly! That was the word she'd been looking for. Wayne looked sly.

"Thanks, but I've already been down to the beach. Funnily enough, I thought I saw you down there too, Wayne," Vanessa said carefully.

"Must have been my alter ego, then, 'cause I've only just gotten back from my bike ride," Wayne said pompously. He turned to his mother. "Can I have more lasagna, Mom? It's really good."

Vanessa was thrown for a moment. Maybe she'd gotten Wayne all wrong. How embarrassing! It wouldn't be the first time she had misread someone.

"Thanks, Wayne," Vanessa said quickly. "Maybe you could show me some other places around here too."

"Maybe," Wayne replied airily, without looking at her, "if you're nice."

CHAPTER 6

Fisherman David Miller from Vancouver Island saw an unknown creature in the sea in November 1959. He said that "other fishermen friends have also reported strange creatures much resembling the one we saw, but are reluctant to report it to the papers or authorities because of the ridicule which follows such sightings."

Vanessa had gone to her bedroom after lunch with the idea of reading her book but had fallen asleep the minute she lay down. She was woken by a knock on the door and staggered off the bed to answer it, feeling like she had been run over by a convoy of trucks. So much for a refreshing nap.

"Would you like to come into town to collect the groceries, Vanessa?" Frankie said when Vanessa opened her bedroom door. She was wheezing badly from the climb up the stairs. "I'll be downstairs," she said without waiting for Vanessa to answer, making her way heavily back down.

Frankie really wasn't able for those stairs. Why hadn't she sent Wayne up? Vanessa wondered. Maybe he had gone out again and it was only Mrs. Bouche who was going into town, she thought with some relief.

Vanessa went to retrieve her runners, which she had left by the back door on her way from the beach at lunchtime. She had forgotten her socks, and when she thrust her bare foot into the shoe something sharp dug into the sole of her foot and made her cry out. Vanessa turned her shoe upside down and a pile of sharp little stones fell out. She stared. How strange! The second shoe was just the same.

She was sure that the stones hadn't been in her shoes when she'd come up for lunch. She couldn't have worn them back from the beach like that. But how else could they have ended up there? That little snake Wayne must have done it! Vanessa flung down her shoes in annoyance. So much for giving him the benefit of the doubt.

As she gathered the stones up, Vanessa toyed with the idea of not going to the village, just in case Wayne was going too. But she couldn't let that little monster get the better of her so easily. Besides, there was absolutely nothing else to do, and she still had hours to kill before Lee came home. It would be a relief to get out and see a bit of the island. Between the rain falling and the bags blocking her view yesterday, she'd seen nothing. Yesterday? It was hard to believe that they had arrived less than twenty-four hours ago. It felt like a lifetime to Vanessa already.

She decided to go.

Wayne sat in the front of the car and chatted away. He pointed out various local landmarks as they drove.

"That's the mill, and over there, just beyond that, is Bear's Head Forest. And see up there on the ridge?" Wayne stuck his finger out of the open window. "They're arbutus trees."

Vanessa looked at them. In the distance, they didn't look like much.

"Arbutus trees are really rare," Wayne said.

Vanessa allowed herself the luxury of turning to the window and rolling her eyes. If she heard another word about their flipping arbutus trees or their fresh air, she would scream. Here she was with a ten-year-old from hell whose mother thought he was a little god, while Lee was . . . Where was Lee? She was only a few miles away with a bunch of scientists discussing Vanessa's favorite creatures in the whole wide world—whales, the giants of the sea. It wasn't fair!

Vanessa gazed at the back of Wayne's head and imagined it inside the mouth of a gigantic killer whale, his legs sticking out, kicking frantically as he was being taken down to the bottom of the ocean. Imagining them was as close as she was going to get to whales on Duquette Island, Vanessa thought bitterly.

Before long, Frankie pulled into the gas station. Attached to the station was a small store. "Givney's Food Emporium" was written above the door on a hand-painted wooden sign.

"That's our church hall," Mrs. Bouche said proudly, pointing to a clapboard building on the opposite side of the road. "Farther up is a gift shop for tourists and all our local crafts are displayed there."

"And then at the top of the hill, near the ferry, is Jo-Jo's," Wayne said eagerly.

Jo-Jo's, at last.

"It's the new ice-cream shop that opened just last summer," Frankie explained. "Lettie runs it. She's away yesterday and today, otherwise we'd go for an ice-cream soda and you could meet her."

"An ice-cream shop on such a small island? That's amazing!" Vanessa exclaimed. "Where do you go to school, Wayne?" she asked then. She'd been imagining the local children crowding into the ice-cream shop after school.

Wayne turned in the front seat and scowled at her.

"There's no school here," his mother said. "Too few kids. But there's one on Granta Island that Wayne used to go to. He doesn't anymore, though. Not since . . ." Frankie hesitated. "These days, Reverend Took takes him for classes two mornings a week."

Wayne's scowl deepened. Clearly Reverend Took was not a favorite with Wayne either.

"Next year I'm going to Vancouver to school," Wayne said loudly, and Vanessa caught the darting look of concern that his mother gave him, although she said nothing. Family webs were always full of dark corners and fragile threads.

Givney's Food Emporium consisted of a small, dimly lit room with a single aisle down the middle. Mrs. Bouche introduced Vanessa to the man and woman behind the counter. Another couple of people came in and were also introduced. Givney's was obviously a key part of island life.

When they heard that Vanessa had come all the way from Ireland, everyone was delighted, and every single one claimed to have Irish-born relatives, although none had ever visited Ireland.

Vanessa and Mrs. Bouche packed the food into the backseat of the car, as the trunk was still full of gardening stuff, and began the ten-minute journey back to the guesthouse.

When they arrived back, Vanessa headed up to her room to wait for Lee. The day felt never-ending. It was three o'clock. Lee had said to Frankie that she would be home in the afternoon, so she probably wouldn't be too much longer. It would be great to find out more about the research center and the missing whales.

When she turned the corner on the landing, Vanessa was surprised to see Wayne in the middle of the doorway to her bedroom, blocking her entrance. He was standing with his feet apart and his hands on his hips, Peter Pan-style, but there was no way he was flying anywhere. Wayne's chunky shoulders and sturdy legs reminded Vanessa of an aggressive little bull.

"What's up, Wayne?" Vanessa said cheerfully.

Wayne didn't answer and he made no effort to move.

"Excuse me, please," Vanessa said with exaggerated politeness.

Wayne stared defiantly back.

Vanessa's eyes narrowed. "Get out of the way, you moron," she growled.

Growling usually worked with her brothers at home, but it didn't appear to be working now. Wayne didn't move. He didn't even blink—that was the snake in him.

"I'm not going anywhere until you promise to be nice to me," Wayne said calmly, his head cocked to one side, an eyebrow raised. "I'll tell my mother if you don't."

Vanessa laughed, part in amusement and part in disbelief. But when she caught the steely flint in Wayne's eyes, she realized that he wasn't messing. He was almost a full foot shorter than she was and his cheeky face made him look like a comical character out of a book, but there was still something menacing about him. He was only ten and he was already a bully.

He tapped his foot impatiently on the floor.

"Well?" he said in a lazy drawl.

Vanessa laughed again. This time she exaggerated her laugh and met Wayne's eyes full on, challenging him. Wayne would be no match for a girl who stood up to him. Vanessa had brothers, and she knew how to fight. It was time to put the poison dwarf in his place.

The whole thing took no more than a couple of seconds. She barely had time to register Wayne pinching his own forearm hard in a couple of places, screaming out in agony and then dropping to the floor, sobbing. It was no more than a few rapid heartbeats before his mother puffed her way up the stairs and stood opposite them, panting.

"Pickles, Pickles, sweetheart, what on earth has happened to you?"

It was unfortunate that Vanessa, amused by the nickname Pickles, should be smiling when Wayne's mother looked up at her.

"She . . . she pinched me. Look!"

Wayne held out his arm where two large angry red welts had appeared.

"I did not!" Vanessa said hotly. Why was this boy being so horrible to her? She'd done nothing to him. "He did that to himself."

The hurt look on Frankie's face hit Vanessa hard, and she turned bright red.

"I did not pinch him!" she said indignantly. "Look! He's grinning at me behind your back," she added, making the situation worse.

Up to this, Vanessa had assumed that Wayne was just overindulged and spoiled, but now she wasn't so sure. If eyes were the mirrors to the soul and all that, then Wayne was in a pretty bad place.

It was hard to know what would have happened next if Lee hadn't walked up the stairs at that very moment. Vanessa was caught between the desire to defend herself and to run away. But where to? Run outside? Step over Wayne and into her bedroom?

Lee raised her eyebrows in question. She opened her mouth to say something but her words were drowned as Wayne's sobs rose a decibel in recognition of his growing audience.

CHAPTER 7

In November 1947 George W. Saggers, a fisherman from Vancouver Island, saw a strange creature while he was salmon fishing. His account appeared in the American magazine *Fate*. "On the port side, about 150 feet away, was a head and neck raised about four feet above the water, with two jet black eyes about three inches across and protruding from the head like buns, staring at me."

Lee sighed as she surveyed the scene at the top of the stairs. Wayne lay on the floor, weeping theatrically; Frankie Bouche looked as if she were about to cry;

and Vanessa had a defiant and furious face on her. The whole scenario made the idea of tracking down illegal whale hunters look like a picnic in comparison.

"Why don't we go downstairs and chat about this?" Lee said calmly, looking at Mrs. Bouche for some adult support.

"Absolutely, Lee," she said immediately. "I think the children have just gotten a bit overwrought."

Vanessa felt her face flame red hot. Children. Overwrought. How dare she!

"I think I'll just wait in my room," Vanessa said through gritted teeth. "I was on my way in there when I suddenly decided to attack Wayne for no reason at all," she added tartly, slamming the bedroom door behind her.

Vanessa threw herself onto her bed and hit the mattress with her fists. The dust plumed in the air.

The rotten little worm! "A five-star pain in the neck!" she said loudly, hoping that they were still outside the door and would hear her.

She should have thumped him rather than try to talk him around. Then at least he'd have had a reason to cry. All things considered, she had been highly restrained all day.

Downstairs, he was probably telling Lee all sorts of lies about her. Maybe she should have gone down rather than just turning tail? Lee didn't even know about the other things Wayne had done—spying on her and putting stones in her shoes. Vanessa had no proof, and it was only a gut feeling, but she just knew she was right.

After about ten minutes there was still no sign of Lee.

Vanessa got up off the bed and went to the window. Instead of opening it, she rested her forehead against the cool glass. She often did that at home when she was upset or needed to think.

She couldn't believe it. After all the trouble she'd had getting here—convincing Lee that it was a good idea, and then her dad—after all that, an irritating ten-year-old was going to spoil the whole trip. Perhaps coming to Duquette Island had been a big mistake.

A gentle knock on her door made her jump. The door opened slowly, and Lee's head appeared around it. Vanessa was relieved that Lee was smiling.

"Sorted," she said brightly. "Get on your swimsuit. We're going for a dip."

"Now?" Vanessa said doubtfully. "But the water's freezing."

"Yup," Lee said briskly. "Bring a towel and a robe for after," she called through the open door. "I'm just going to change."

CHAPTER 8

The whale wavered and towered motionless above us. I looked up past the daggered six-inch teeth into a massive eye, an eye that reflected back an intelligence, an eye that spoke wordlessly of compassion . . . on that day I knew emotionally and spiritually that my allegiance lay with the whale first and foremost over the interests of humans that would kill them.

—Paul Watson, antiwhaling activist

Vanessa changed quickly. She wanted to ask Lee what she had meant by "sorted." Sorted as in Lee had apologized on her behalf? Or sorted as in Wayne was lying on the kitchen floor with a stake through his heart?

Vanessa warned Lee about the broken tiles and the gaps in the steps to the beach. Luckily there was still plenty of light and they navigated their way down the steps easily enough.

As Lee and Vanessa walked on the beach they listened to the noisy chatter of the insects all around them. It was like there was some huge insect beach party and they had kindly agreed to provide all the food and drink, Vanessa remarked, and Lee laughed. It wasn't cold out, but Vanessa was glad she had worn her robe because the long sleeves at least prevented her arms from getting eaten.

"The sooner we get in the water the better. Last in . . ." Lee said, draping her robe over a rock and hobbling across the stones to the water's edge.

Lee was a pretty woman who looked much younger than her forty-three years. Because she tended to wear high heels, she gave the impression of being tall, and Vanessa was surprised now to find that they were almost the same height. In every other way, however, they were opposites, and there was little chance of mistaking them for mother and daughter. While Lee was blonde, fair, and neat, Vanessa had a mop of black wavy hair, olive skin, and very long limbs. Her older brother, Luke, always teased her about being lanky. Vanessa hoped that she would stop growing soon and become more normally proportioned. She'd love to have a nice figure rather than looking like a stick.

Vanessa walked quickly into the sea, right up to her waist, and gasped with the shock of the cold on her skin. She looked around for Lee, but she was entirely submerged.

There was no going back now. Vanessa went headfirst under the next small wave. When she stood up to catch her breath, Lee was standing beside her.

"Stay under, Vanessa. Put your head in the water—quick," Lee said urgently before disappearing again under the surface of the choppy gray water.

Vanessa took a deep breath and plunged in. At first she noticed only the sudden lack of sound, the off-switch for the insect racket, and then she heard it: a slow, high-pitched musical whine, followed by a deep, reassuring groan. The doleful sound went on for ages and Vanessa, who was almost bursting from holding her breath, shot up out of the water.

"Whales! Oh my God, Lee—the whales! Did you hear the whales?"

Lee was grinning broadly at her, and Vanessa realized how stupid she sounded. Of course Lee knew about the whales. That was why she had suggested a swim in the first place. The cetacean laboratory was on a neighboring island because the whales came to these waters at this time of year.

"It's probably a humpback whale," Lee said. "Males and females can vocalize, but it's only the males that sing the song. It can last for ages—up to forty minutes."

Vanessa plunged back under. She'd ask questions later. It was just so exciting knowing these 50-foot giants were nearby and that she was listening to them.

The sounds came from every direction and were so clear that Vanessa felt a whale might pop up beside her any minute. Surround sound at its very best. Tomorrow she'd find a snorkel and a mask so that she could stay under as long as she liked. Maybe she'd even swim out a bit.

Vanessa was shivering uncontrollably by the time she finally agreed to get out of the water. She felt elated as she dried herself off, as if she had made a discovery, a connection of some sort. She found it difficult to get her dressing gown on and almost impossible to tie the belt. Her whole body felt like her face did after a visit to the dentist.

"How did it go today at work?" she asked Lee, her words slurred through numbed lips.

"OK," Lee said noncommittally.

Before Vanessa could ask anything more, a rustling behind them in the bushes stopped them in their tracks. They stared at each other for a moment, wide-eyed. There it was again.

"Just a bird or a cat," Lee finally said dismissively.

The rustling stopped, and Lee started to walk toward the steps to go back up, but Vanessa wanted to investigate. Picking up a long stick, she poked at the shrubbery.

"Come on, Vanessa," Lee called. "It's probably some poor little raccoon and you're scaring the wits out of him."

Vanessa knew the creature all right. It was Wayne, eavesdropping again, and she felt sick to her stomach at the thought that he had been watching and listening to them.

"Come on, Vanessa," Lee shouted again. "It's freezing."

Vanessa decided to say nothing about her Wayne theory. Lee would probably think she was being paranoid.

She followed Lee slowly up the steps, her thoughts entirely taken up with Wayne. They were due to stay at Rocky Bay for at least another six days. What on earth was she going to do about Wayne? Even the memory of the wonderful whale singing couldn't cheer her up now.

It wasn't until Vanessa was back in her bed, snuggled up under her warm duvet and behind a locked door, that she remembered what Lee had said: "Sorted!"

Sorted, my foot. Clearly it was far from sorted.

CHAPTER 9

Witnesses consistently describe the sea monster as a giant reptilian creature with coils or humps, a strangely shaped head (like a horse or cow), and bulging black eyes. Its face has been described as both "horrific" and "loveable."

It was hot and steamy. Vanessa found it hard to suck the air into her lungs. Looking down, she saw that there were large rubbery leaves stuck to her skin and covering most of her body. It wasn't a leaf she recognized. She crouched down into the bushes, uncertain what to do. Just then a little furry snake appeared and told her to peel the leaves off quickly or she would die. Vanessa was surprised that the snake's voice was so high and squeaky, but she did as it said and started to pull off a leaf. It was a slow and painful process, but she was delighted to see that it left a beautiful green vein pattern on her skin. She gazed with pleasure at the fine branches dividing and subdividing and looked around to show the snake, but it was gone. All she could hear now was its rattle, and it was getting louder. A warning sign. Danger.

She should be moving. But her legs and arms just wouldn't budge. Rattle, rattle . . . rattle, rattle . . . It was close enough to strike. Close enough to . . .

"Vanessa? Vanessa! Are you OK in there?"

Vanessa rose to the surface. Still befuddled from sleep, she turned her head slowly to look at her arms. Alas, no leaf tattoos. The rattle began again and she saw that the handle of her bedroom door was being twisted back and forth. Vaguely relieved that it wasn't a rattlesnake, but still not conscious enough to wonder at the rattling door, she closed her eyes again.

"Vanessa, there's something I have to tell you before I leave this morning."

Vanessa's brain finally engaged and she struggled to her feet.

"Thought that touch of hypothermia you got last night might have finished you off," Lee said when Vanessa unlocked the door.

"Sorry, I was in a deep sleep, having wild dreams," Vanessa said. "Thought you were a rattlesnake. Wonder if there are any on the island. Might go out and look for some later." She was still only half-awake.

Lee laughed. "You're busy today, actually."

Vanessa perked up instantly.

"Mr. Fox is going to take you out whale-watching in the boat after he drops me off." She smiled at Vanessa, expecting oohs and aahs, but Vanessa stared back uncomprehendingly.

"Mr. Fox?" she said at last. "After he drops you off?"

"Yes," Lee said slowly, watching Vanessa's face. "He's going to drop me to Brighton Island, to the research station, as he did yesterday, but today he'll come back and take you to Wilbur Sound or Governor Bay, whichever is the best place to see the whales at that time. . . ." Lee's voice trailed off. Then she asked, "Can I come in for a moment?"

Lee walked into the bedroom and shut the door behind her.

"What's the matter, Vanessa? I thought you would be thrilled."

Vanessa sat on the side of her bed and stared down at her hands. She was furiously trying to order her thoughts. She wanted to say she was pleased about the whale-watching, but she just couldn't work up the enthusiasm right now. Wayne was the matter, really, but she didn't want to sound whiny, complaining about him again.

"Who is Mr. Fox?" she said at last.

Lee looked surprised and then gave a small apologetic laugh.

"I'm sorry, Vanessa. With the full-scale theatrical performance from Wayne and then going swimming, I just forgot to tell you last night. Mr. Fox is my driver. Or in this case my captain, as we have to use a boat to get to the research station."

"You mean he works for Greenpeace too?"

"No. I mean he helps out at the research laboratory sometimes, getting supplies and ferrying people about. I've hired him for the week to help me." Lee spoke in a low, calm voice. "What's the problem, Vanessa?"

"Nothing really. You just hadn't mentioned him before, that's all. I'd have remembered the name Fox for sure."

"I'm sorry, Vanessa," Lee said, although the tone of her voice didn't make it sound like an apology. "It's habit with me, I suppose. I'm not used to having a teenager with me when I work, that's all."

Vanessa didn't look up.

"As a rule," Lee continued, "I don't talk about my job very much. I've already told you that this is a sensitive matter, and the less people know the better." She paused, waiting for Vanessa to look up. "Frankie and Wayne would love to get hold of any gossip there might be, and I don't need any more drama, do I?"

Vanessa stood up and hugged Lee.

"Sorry, Lee," she said with feeling. "I'm just being silly. Of course I'd love to go out with Mr. Fox. I'll find a snorkel and I'll bring my sketchbook. Maybe I could get a loan of a wetsuit. Maybe the little monster downstairs would have one. It wouldn't matter if it's too short."

"Ah, yes. About Wayne." Lee's voice dropped, and Vanessa guessed there was something else coming. "The only way I could think to sort the little problem yesterday was to invite Wayne to go out whale-watching with Mr. Fox too." Lee's voice was full of apology this time. "Mrs. Bouche—Frankie—seemed to think it would be great for you both. That it would help iron out your differences."

Vanessa gave a hard little laugh. It would take more than a boat ride to do that. Should she tell Lee now about his spying on her and the stones in her shoes? What if Lee didn't believe her? Better not. Maybe Wayne had done his worst already and he'd be better when he was away from his mother. She'd just have to get through it and enjoy it as best she could, she decided.

"Oh, we'll be fine together," she said breezily. "Hopefully he'll fall overboard and a whale will crush him or something."

CHAPTER 10

On a Sunday morning in December 1933, Cyril Andrews and Norman Georgeson saw Caddy while they were duck hunting near South Pender Island. They called in the Justice of the Peace, Mr. G. F. Parkyn, who took down a sworn statement of what they had seen. About ten minutes later the creature appeared again close to the shore, and eleven people, including Mr. Parkyn, witnessed it.

Vanessa got dressed and went down to breakfast. She felt a little anxious but she wasn't sure why. Most likely it was the thought of spending the day with Wayne.

As she walked through the house, Vanessa couldn't help noticing that the place, although tidy and clean, looked a bit shabby and definitely in need of a lick of paint. There were no pictures on the walls, but there were photographs in silver frames everywhere—over the fireplace, on the piano, on the bookshelves. Vanessa stopped to examine them. They were mostly of the same three people: Frankie, slimmer and looking younger; Wayne as a chubby toddler; and a tall, thin man with gray hair who had a lovely warm smile. Frankie's husband, probably.

Frankie was in top form at breakfast. She told Vanessa all about her parents and how they had started the guesthouse over forty years ago. There was no gap in the conversation, and Vanessa could only gawp at the rising pile of pancakes.

"Honestly, Frankie, I've heaps," Vanessa murmured finally, putting her hand over her plate.

"By the way, honey, I've got an extra wetsuit for you," Frankie announced. "It may be a little big, but Lee thought it would be better than nothing."

"Oh, that's great, Frankie," Vanessa said. "Thanks so much."

"Wayne has his own, of course. He's an exceptional

swimmer. Not surprising, I suppose, given that he lives on an island and that his father is a famous free diver in these parts."

"What's free diving, Frankie?"

"I suppose you might say it's deepwater diving without the scuba gear; not even fins—you go as deep as you can in one breath. Dangerous if you don't train properly for it."

"How deep can he go?" Vanessa asked.

"His record is 170 feet. But the best in the world is about 335."

"Wow, that's incredible! I'd say ten feet would be my tops!"

"Wayne will be just as good as his father, I expect. He's got big lungs for his age and can hold his breath for over a minute already."

It would have been a perfect moment to ask whether the man in the photos was Wayne's dad, but Vanessa was suddenly caught by a fit of the giggles at the idea of Wayne's big lungs. She coughed to hide her amusement and then had to keep coughing when Frankie began to tap her on the back.

"A glass of water?" Vanessa begged huskily in between coughs and splutters.

When she had recovered, she helped Frankie to clear the table.

"Here you go – wetsuit, flippers, snorkel, and lunch," Frankie said, handing Vanessa a large straw bag. "I've put in plenty of snacks and drinks for you both and some nice chicken salad rolls."

She smiled so eagerly that Vanessa felt bad again briefly. But the feeling didn't last long. Wayne strutted into the room, dressed in his wetsuit, complete with flippers, mask, and goggles.

"Aren't you ready yet?" he said rudely.

Vanessa turned away, pulling a face, and found herself looking straight into the face of a small wiry man with a neatly trimmed mustache. It had to be Mr. Fox.

After the introductions had been made, Mr. Fox told them that his boat was moored in the next bay. It was a ten-minute walk along the stony beach, so they should wear comfortable, nonslip shoes. Wayne changed out of his flippers and, to Vanessa's relief, chatted away quite normally to Mr. Fox as they walked to the boat. He didn't whine once.

Vanessa found that she wasn't really included in the conversation, so she dropped back a little to observe Mr. Fox better. She smiled. He did actually walk a bit like a fox. As he made his way quickly along the stony beach he looked agile and careful. In contrast, Wayne stomped beside him, stumbling in an effort to keep up. She wondered if Mr. Fox lived on Duquette Island and how well he knew Wayne.

Vanessa felt a flutter of excitement in the pit of her stomach when she saw the boat for the first time. It was much bigger than she had imagined. More like a small trawler, although there were no fishing lines or nets visible. There was even a rubber dinghy tied up on the beach to allow them to get out to it. A tender, Mr. Fox said it was called.

Vanessa would have been very happy with just the tender, although they would get much farther out in the trawler and there would be no possibility of a whale turning them over. She had read about things like that happening. In fact, a little part of her secretly wouldn't have minded. She'd swum with something just as big in Loch Ness before and loved it!

When they got onto the trawler, Mr. Fox handed them each a life jacket immediately.

"Feel free to wander around the boat," he said, "but you must wear the life jackets at all times and you must not stand on or lean over the rails. Understood?"

He turned sharply, not expecting an answer, and went back down the steps to the tender.

"I'm just going to tie the tender to the mooring buoy and then we'll set off," he called over his shoulder.

"Can I help?" Vanessa asked.

"You can if you can tie a decent bowline, little lady," Mr. Fox said.

Little lady? Her brothers would laugh. That was something she wasn't used to being called.

"It's lucky I can, then." She grinned up at him. "Reef, half-hitch, bowline."

Mr. Fox didn't try to hide his surprise. "Wow. I guess your education system in Europe ain't so fancy after all. Pretty hands-on, huh?"

"If only," Vanessa said wistfully. "I learnt none of that in school. All on the Internet—like everything else useful in life."

In the last couple of years Vanessa had, with the help of YouTube and various minority-interest websites, taught herself the art of knot-tying, which was followed by an intensive study of Morse code and, more recently, sign language.

"I can tie all the knots she can," Wayne piped up.

Poor Wayne, Vanessa thought. He was just a baby, really, desperate to be the center of attention.

The tender was tied up to the buoy with Vanessa's bowline, which was checked and duly admired by Mr. Fox.

"You haven't skippered a fishing trawler before, I suppose?" Mr. Fox said with a grin, as they walked back to the bridge.

"Not yet," Vanessa replied.

"Let's go to Governor Bay first. I saw a mother and her baby there on my way back from Brighton half an hour ago," Mr. Fox said to Vanessa. "Where's Wayne?" he said suddenly, scanning the boat. "He can't be gone overboard already, surely. WAYNE!" he yelled.

"I'm here," Wayne called back, still not visible. "Just checking the tender," he said, climbing back up the last step onto the deck of the trawler.

"Good man," Mr. Fox said hurriedly, throwing a glance at the little boat. "OK, let's go."

CHAPTER 11

The humpback whale is the fifth-largest animal on the planet. An adult weighs the same as eleven elephants, and yet they are the most acrobatic of all of the great whales, famous for breaching (jumping almost completely out of the water).

The waves slapped against the bow of the boat as it cut through the water. Vanessa leaned into the wind. This was wonderful.

Lee had said that the North Pacific whales were beginning to migrate up from the warm waters of

Hawaii to spend the summer here, and that later in the summer there would be many more. Fingers crossed that they would actually see a whale up close today.

They motored for about twenty minutes before Mr. Fox cut the engines.

"It was around here that I saw them. Sometimes they'll hang around for a bit if they are feeding. Keep watching out and you might see them blow."

Almost immediately, Wayne let out a shriek.

"Look, I see one!" he said, pointing toward the stern of the boat.

Wayne, of course, would have to be the first to see a whale.

They moved quickly to the stern of the boat and waited. Vanessa held her breath and scanned the water, waiting for the large gray back to break the surface.

"I did see one," Wayne insisted when nothing appeared.

"It's probably gone down, Wayne," Mr. Fox said. He turned to Vanessa. "They can hold their breath for half an hour or more, so they can be miles away by the time they surface again."

After another five minutes, Mr. Fox started the engines again and they moved off slowly.

Vanessa felt a deep and satisfying delight at the scowl on Wayne's face, but she managed not to crow.

Face to the wind, they resumed their journey, while Mr. Fox pointed out the various islands and bays named after the English and Spanish explorers who arrived in the eighteenth century.

"Before that point, it was a scattering of remote islands in the middle of nowhere. The Europeans brought civilization to the place and tried to educate the natives," Mr. Fox said seriously.

The way he said it made Vanessa feel very uncomfortable. Wasn't that just like the Spanish conquistadors who wiped out the Aztecs, or the Europeans who did the same to the aboriginal tribes in Australia?

"I don't think they treated them very well, though, did they?" she said quietly, not at all sure she should be saying anything, but unable to stop herself.

Mr. Fox looked mildly surprised and then smiled at her. "You're right, of course," he agreed. "Sometimes when we look back, progress can seem a bit ruthless even though it's necessary."

Necessary? For what? For whom? Not the native

peoples who had been living here, that was for sure. Vanessa opened her mouth to argue, but Wayne cut across her.

"I'm hungry," he whined. "You shouldn't hog the lunch bag, Vanessa. Frankie meant us to share."

Vanessa shoved the bag at him.

"Have as much as you like, Wayne," she said through gritted teeth. "Just don't choke on the sandwiches," she added, dropping her voice.

Wayne eyed her solemnly. "You know, you're a very cranky person," he said loudly.

Luckily Mr. Fox intervened before the argument could escalate further.

"Up ahead, starboard side," he called urgently, pointing to the right. He turned the boat and then picked up speed.

At first Vanessa could see nothing. Then in the distance she saw a fin appear out of the water, hesitate for a second, and begin slapping the surface of the water.

"He's pec slapping," Mr. Fox shouted over the noise of the engine.

Vanessa laughed. It looked so playful, like a toddler slapping the water in a bathtub.

As they got closer, Mr. Fox cut the engines, and immediately a huge gray back broke the surface and rolled gracefully. Then another appeared beside it.

Vanessa gasped. Their size was incredible, and the sight of them so close blew her mind. She really felt as if she was in the presence of something important, something prehistoric.

"They're humpback whales, probably males. See the one waving his tail at us? That means either he's going straight down and will disappear or—"

Mr. Fox didn't have time to finish before the whale shot up vertically out of the water and landed on its back with a thunderous crash and a huge splash. "Or he'll breach," Mr. Fox finished with a grin.

"Oh my God!" Vanessa exclaimed. She had seen it on wildlife programs, but this wasn't the same. The thunderous noise, the beauty of their movement, the power needed to jump so high. It was breathtaking.

"Imagine," Vanessa whispered to herself. "I'm in British Columbia, watching humpbacks play right in front of me." When Vanessa did this, it was the mental equivalent of pinching herself. Not only did it help her mark the moment as a permanent memory, but she actually enjoyed the words themselves: the foreignness of them thrilled her—British Columbia, humpbacks—it was so unbelievable.

She had forgotten about Wayne.

"Why are you talking to yourself, Vanessa?" Wayne said loudly. "It's the first sign of madness, you know."

He grinned slyly at her, and Vanessa could have sworn he gave a conspiratorial wink to Mr. Fox.

"Shut up, you little twit," Vanessa said irritably. Wayne really could spoil any occasion.

Mr. Fox looked at her sharply.

"Sorry," she said quickly. "Tetchy because I'm tired. Dreamt about people hiding in bushes and eavesdropping," she added pointedly.

This caused Wayne to grin even harder.

Just as Vanessa turned away, she thought she saw Mr. Fox give Wayne a little nod. Vanessa stared. Were they up to something? No, she scolded herself, she was being silly. She really needed to calm down a bit and not let Wayne get to her.

The whales, which had disappeared for a while, now surfaced again. They were even closer this time, cutting across the bow of the stationary boat, their backs rising and submerging in the water, spray billowing from their spout holes. And then the magic happened—a third, tiny whale swam out from beneath the larger one.

"Look, there's a baby!" Wayne shouted.

"Oh my God, a whole family," Vanessa said wistfully. Tears sprang unexpectedly to her eyes, taking her by surprise. She wiped them away quickly before they could get a hold. Luckily it was windy.

"Humpbacks don't tend to travel in families," Mr. Fox said. "It's usually the mother and the baby with another female. The males travel in packs. Bit like humans, I suppose," he added with a smirk.

The whales swam around the boat for a while, the baby swimming beneath the mother, the companion staying close. Vanessa wondered what it would be like to swim with the whales.

As she watched they sank slowly, as one, beneath the surface. It was only then that Vanessa noticed that Mr. Fox was speaking quietly into the handset of the radio. Vanessa strained to hear what he was saying, but the sound of Wayne munching his way through a bag of potato chips made it impossible.

CHAPTER 12

In January 1992 Dorothy Sinclair saw a monster in Gray's Harbor. "The long slender neck rose, I would say, five or six feet in the air, and the thing that struck me was that incredible dignity!"

"Maybe we'll move on and find some others," Mr. Fox suggested finally. He started the engine. "I think we'll head up to Gray's Harbor. It's a nice place if you want to go for a swim. You can change into your wetsuit in the cabin if you like, Vanessa."

Vanessa put on the wetsuit and then ate her chicken

roll before Wayne could polish off everything in the bag. All the snacks and treats were gone already, she noticed, and the fizzy drinks too. There was just a single bottle of water left, but Vanessa didn't really mind. The whales were all that mattered.

Mr. Fox cut the engine as they approached an inlet.

"Think I'll make a cup of coffee and have something to eat too," he said. "Don't get into the water until I'm ready."

Vanessa went to the back of the boat and looked up at the craggy cliffs and the strangely deformed-looking trees that clung to the edges. Then a sudden movement in the water caught her eye. There was something moving just below the surface. Could it be another whale?

Vanessa froze. Not a whale. What on earth was it?

She could make out a long neck and a large head just under the surface. A moray eel? A huge bird diving for fish? The creature submerged fully and Vanessa sighed heavily. Now she'd never know.

"Did you see something?" Mr. Fox called out to Vanessa.

"Just a bird," she called back, as casually as she could, although her heart was thumping in her chest. There was something moving in the water again. It was back, whatever it was!

Vanessa gripped the handrail and stared. What was it? A seal didn't have a long neck like that. And the head! She'd never seen anything like it before. It was extraordinary—like a horse's head with its nose squished in.

Vanessa froze as the creature turned, and she saw its bulging black eyes and two small bumps near the top of its head. Ears? Horns? Her camera was in her backpack, but she didn't dare move in case she missed anything.

"You've seen something back there, haven't you?" Wayne called to her from the front, making her start.

At that very moment, the creature moved a little in the water and Vanessa saw a number of large humps—no, not humps, really—more like the vertical coils of a giant snake as it moves.

Whatever happened, Vanessa knew she couldn't let Wayne see it. She pulled a coin out of her pocket and threw it as hard as she could at the creature. She didn't know whether she had hit it or not, but it suddenly darted away, quick and agile as an eel, and then disappeared.

"What are you up to?" Wayne said suspiciously, joining her at the rail and peering down into the water where the creature had just been.

Vanessa's mouth was so dry that she croaked the word. "Money," she said, clearing her throat.

"Throwing money into the sea?" Wayne said with mock outrage. "You're just weird, Vanessa."

It was the first time that he had used her name, and she didn't like it at all.

"It's for luck," Vanessa said quickly, praying the creature wouldn't reappear. "It's an old fisherman's tradition we have in Ireland."

She turned and walked away, hoping that Wayne would follow her.

He did.

"That's just stupid," he said.

"A lot of traditions are, I suppose. The Chookinan tribe in this part of the world used to drown their firstborn boy, didn't they?" Vanessa's eyes narrowed as she lied. She had no idea if there was such a tribe and knew nothing about native practices. "That would have been you gone, Wayne," she said with emphasis.

Wayne's mouth opened and closed, but he said nothing, and Vanessa grinned. One point for her. Or so she thought, until she noticed Mr. Fox watching her. Why was she always the one to get caught out?

CHAPTER 13

In October 1937 at Naden Harbor Whaling Station, whalers cut open the stomach of a sperm whale and found the 20-foot long carcass of an unidentifiable creature. It was described as having a horselike head, a serpentine body, and a finned, spiny tail. Although it is not known what happened to the carcass, there are three photographs still in existence. To this day no scientist has been able to identify the creature.

In the end, neither Vanessa nor Wayne felt like going for a swim. The water had turned quite choppy and cold, so Mr. Fox started the engines, deciding that they should head home.

Vanessa was subdued and silent. Her thoughts returned obsessively to the image of the coils, the bulging eyes, and the extraordinary head. She had only seen the creature for a few seconds, she guessed, but what she had seen had turned her whole world on its head.

Could she have been hallucinating? A food allergy? Was there a strange marine creature in this part of the world that she had never heard about?

"Besides whales, what else do you get in these waters? Anything weird and wonderful in this part of the world?" she asked Mr. Fox eventually.

"Seals, sea lions, porpoises mainly."

"Don't think so," Vanessa said doubtfully. Mr. Fox gave her a funny look.

"Don't think what?" Wayne asked.

"Nothing. I just saw a strange-looking bird on the water," Vanessa replied lamely.

"Maybe you're seeing things, Vanessa," Wayne said slyly. "That's the second sign of madness, you know."

His round eyes in his moon face met hers. Vanessa didn't react, but his words hit home hard. Maybe she was a bit loopy. She did sometimes see things that other people didn't.

"You seasick?" Mr. Fox asked Vanessa.

"No. Not at all," Vanessa replied, surprised by the question, unaware of how pale she was looking.

"See the land in the distance there, Vanessa? That's Brighton Island." He looked quickly at Wayne, who was playing with some ropes in the middle of the boat, and lowered his voice a little. "That's where Lee is working."

Normally, Vanessa would have been full of questions.

"That's great," she said flatly.

She stared out at the horizon, but she kept thinking about the creature in the water. She was coming slowly to the conclusion that she might just have witnessed another cryptid. But which cryptid? What was its name, and would it be in her mum's files in the attic at home? How was she going to work this one out?

CHAPTER 14

Alan Maclean of Vancouver Island saw the sea monster in 1962 and probably regretted ever reporting it. He received joke mail with offers of free eye tests and even membership in Alcoholics Anonymous.

Vanessa was barely conscious of the return journey, and it wasn't until Mr. Fox let out a roar that she was dragged back to the present.

"The tender's gone," he cried, staring at the mooring. "I should have done it myself," he muttered angrily.

Although he dropped his voice, Vanessa still heard him. She felt her stomach turn over. She knew she had tied it up properly—Mr. Fox had even checked the knot. She looked to where it should have been and then scanned the bay frantically. *Please be there, please be there.* But it was nowhere to be seen.

"I'm so sorry, Mr. Fox. I'm sure the knot was good," Vanessa said, trying not to cry.

She knew how important the little tender was. The trawler was too big to bring into the shallows.

"Forget it," Mr. Fox said shortly. "I'll go in as close as I can and let you guys swim in with your wetsuits and snorkels. Then I'll go and look for the tender. OK?"

Wayne was remarkably quiet, and when Vanessa looked at him, he avoided her eyes. That was odd. Not like Wayne to miss a chance to gloat.

Unless . . .

Vanessa struggled to recall the sequence of events. After she'd tied the tender, Mr. Fox had checked it. And then what? Then Wayne went to check it, she remembered now. Had he loosened it deliberately? Why would he do that? To get her into trouble?

"You checked it after we did, didn't you, Wayne?" Vanessa asked him.

"He's ten, Vanessa," Mr. Fox said tersely. "How is he supposed to know a good knot?"

With that, he banged his hand on the railing, and Vanessa could see that he was trying to control his temper. Did he think that Vanessa was trying to shift the blame on to Wayne? She'd have to watch herself. Wayne might be annoying, but he was an islander, and being local would mean a lot around here, she guessed.

"OK, sorry," Vanessa said quickly. "Sounds like a good plan. I hope you find it, Mr. Fox. Come on, Wayne," she added chummily.

"Last one in is a girl," Wayne yelled as they stood at the edge.

Vanessa sighed inwardly as Wayne gave a triumphant shout and jumped in. He swam quickly to the shore, determined to be first. She had to admit that he had a really nice stroke. Maybe his mother hadn't been exaggerating about his swimming abilities after all.

Vanessa swam slowly back to the beach. It would be hard work walking across two stony beaches in her bare feet, but she'd take her time, and that way she'd avoid arriving back with Wayne. Vanessa hoped that Mr. Fox would remember to bring back her runners later; otherwise she'd have nothing to wear tomorrow.

When Vanessa got back to the guesthouse, there was no sign of Wayne or Frankie. Relieved, she crept up the stairs to her bedroom, had a leisurely shower, and then lay down on her bed to read.

When she'd read the same page for the fourth time and still couldn't remember what it was about, she put down her book.

She leaned over the side of her bed and picked up her backpack. She unzipped an internal pocket and took out a small object with great care.

In her hand she held an ugly, puckered shrunken head that was about the size of a small orange. It had long black hair and its lips were stitched shut with twine. The shrunken head had belonged to her grandfather, Todd, an explorer who had lived with a head-shrinking tribe in Ecuador a long time ago. Vanessa had found the head in the attic when she was looking for her mother's cryptid files. Now she took it everywhere with her, told it secrets—and sometimes got advice back!

"You should have seen it, Toddy," Vanessa whispered. "It was like nothing I've ever seen before. I only saw part of its back and it was huge. It was kind of like a cross between a giant snake and a huge crocodile with a horse's face!"

She looked sharply at the head, its face held in a permanent grimace.

"You wouldn't grin like that if you had seen how ugly it was," Vanessa said grimly.

Toddy said nothing.

It was about five o'clock when Mr. Fox returned with Lee. Vanessa met them at the door as they came in. She noticed that Mr. Fox was looking much more cheerful now.

"Good news," he said heartily, presenting Vanessa with her runners. "I found the tender eventually, thank goodness, and Dr. McDonald didn't have to swim in fully clothed."

Lee grinned.

"Where did you find it in the end?" Vanessa asked.

"Not far from Rocky Bay, actually. It must have come off quite quickly after we set off and then drifted a bit. We'll have to have a little refresher course on knots someday soon," Mr. Fox added—rather unnecessarily, Vanessa thought.

Lee put her arm on Vanessa's shoulder and squeezed it.

"Had fun today, then?" she said.

"It was amazing, Lee. They were so huge up close, and so beautiful. There was a baby humpback too," Vanessa said dreamily. "I'd love to be a scientist and study them."

"Tomorrow, I'll ask Dr. Mitchell if you could visit the research lab before we fly out. Just to see the setup—the hydrophones that record the whales singing," Lee said thoughtfully. "He's terribly nice. He runs a graduate fellowship program, which you could do when you're older, Vanessa, if you're interested."

Vanessa's eyes widened in amazement. Lee wasn't like other adults, who were always putting obstacles in the way—you couldn't do this and that. She never treated her like a silly kid, although Vanessa knew that she had been just that when they first met. She cringed now to think of the fuss she'd made about their trip to Loch Ness.

"Would you? Oh, Lee, that would be fantastic," she said gratefully.

Vanessa was dying to ask if it could be tomorrow, but she swallowed her words. Better not to badger Lee.

"Can I go too?" Wayne's whiny voice came from

over Vanessa's left shoulder, and it was all she could do to resist stamping her foot.

"I'll see what I can do, Wayne," Lee said lightly, squeezing Vanessa's forearm again and giving her a conspiratorial grin.

CHAPTER 15

It has been reported that, on 13 February 1953, Caddy was observed by ten people who watched from different viewpoints around Qualicum Bay. Surely this number of people can't all have been mistaken?

Later that evening, Vanessa decided to ring home. It would cost a fortune on her mobile, but she had to call Luke or Ronan and see if they could look at her mum's cryptid files, which were stored in the attic. Her work had been put up there after she died.

But which brother should she call? Luke would be better at finding the files, but he would ask too many questions.

The ringing went on for ages before a small, sleepy voice answered.

"Hullo?"

"Hi, Ronan, it's me. How are you?" Vanessa said.

"Who is this?" Ronan's voice became belligerent.

"It's me, Vanessa, you idiot. Your sister? I've only been gone a few days."

"For God's sake, Vanessa, it's the middle of the night here," Ronan said indignantly.

Whoops. She had totally forgotten about the time difference.

"Sorry, Ro. But I need you to do me a favor. Please, please," Vanessa begged. "I'll never ask you for anything else again and I'll back you up against Dad in the event of a row."

"Wow. Must be big." Ronan sounded more awake now.

"I just need you to go up into the attic for me and find a file." Vanessa tried to sound matter-of-fact.

"You what?"

"Just listen," Vanessa said quickly. "I don't have

enough time or credit to explain fully. I'm looking for a file. It may be in one of Mum's boxes near the trapdoor in the attic. It will be a colored folder and will be about a monster in Canada. . . ."

Her voice trailed away. It sounded odd, even to her.

She felt her heart sink. Would Ronan find it, even if it was there?

"A monster?" Ronan asked in a tired voice. "What are you on about, Vanessa?"

"I'm just following up on some of Mum's research. Pleeeease, Ronan. Do you remember, I brought a folder to Loch Ness that time we went? It will be just like that, but it will be about a creature in Canada. I don't know its name, though."

"OK. A folder about an unknown Canadian monster," he repeated finally. "I'll try to find it. But you're not expecting me to go and get it now, Vanessa?"

"It will only take a couple of minutes, Ro, and you could call me back," she pleaded. "Otherwise I won't get a wink of sleep tonight, wondering."

Vanessa heard him give a grim laugh.

"Good," he said. "Then you'll know how it feels to be sleep-deprived, like me."

"But couldn't you just—"

"Listen to me, Vanessa," Ronan said sternly. "I'll look for it in the morning, so don't you dare call me back before then." He slammed down the phone.

CHAPTER 16

There are reports of the monster being seen on land. In 1936 E. J. Stephenson, with his wife and son, saw a huge unidentifiable creature wriggling over the reef into a lagoon on Saturna Island.

After breakfast the next morning, Vanessa walked with Lee down the beach at the next bay to meet Mr. Fox. Lee hadn't said anything about taking Vanessa with her to Brighton Island that morning, but Vanessa remained hopeful.

"What's the plan today?" Lee asked her as they

waited for Mr. Fox to bring the tender in.

That was disappointing. Clearly, Lee had no intention of taking Vanessa with her.

"Brought my sketchpad and might draw for a bit on the beach," Vanessa said lightly, although she felt gloomy already.

Hide until lunch to avoid Wayne, she said in her head.

After Vanessa waved Lee and Mr. Fox off, she walked farther along the beach and found a pile of huge boulders.

It would be a good place to hide from Wayne and kill a bit of time.

Nestled in the center of the boulders, Vanessa found that she was protected from view on all sides. She just hoped that there weren't any large crabs hiding in there with her.

She took out her charcoal pencil and sketchbook, turned to a fresh page and stared at it. What should she draw? Normally she'd just let her pencil lead her, make quick rough sketches of whatever came into her head. Now she hesitated, and the empty whiteness of the page overwhelmed her. Did the equivalent of writer's block exist for artists?

Maybe the whale music that Lee had loaded onto her iPod would help. She plugged the headphones into her ears and listened, waiting for inspiration. The image of the whale and its huge body breaching came to her. She could hear the thunderous noise, see the almighty splash. She started to draw it. Then she drew herself swimming nearby. Vanessa smiled. She looked tiny by comparison. No wonder whales were called the "giants of the ocean."

She threw her head back, looking skyward, and thought about the strange creature she had seen yesterday. It had looked huge and powerful. Scary too, not at all friendly like Nessie. More like the Chupacabra. An involuntary shiver ran down her spine as she thought back to Mexico and that terrible night she had seen the devilish eyes watching her.

Now her thoughts jumped to Ronan. She wondered if he had gone up to the attic last night, or if he'd gone back to sleep. Would he even find a file? She tried calling him again, but there was no answer.

Vanessa turned over the page. OK. She'd try to draw it, whatever it was. She concentrated hard, trying to recall the head with the funny little bulges and huge eyes. Then she drew the snakelike coils and the misshapen head. The creature started to emerge, but then the nib on her pencil broke. No sharpener either. She tried again with the stub of the pencil but it looked so bad. Like a toddler's drawing of some fantasy animal. Frustrated, Vanessa tore the page out, scrunched it into a ball and pushed it in between two rocks.

Vanessa switched off her iPod and put it back into her bag. For a split second, she thought she heard her name, a distant cry that hung in the air. Then a seagull mewed overhead and she watched it soar higher and higher.

"Vaannessaaaa." This time there was no doubting it. Vanessa poked her head above the level of the rocks and peered about. It could be Wayne trying to trick her.

"Vanessa, where are you?"

It was clearer this time, and Vanessa could tell that it was a woman's voice. Lee?

"Vanessa, you've got to hurry."

Vanessa turned and saw Lee standing beside the tender on the beach, her hands cupped around her mouth.

How come she was back from Brighton Island already? And Mr. Fox's boat was there too. Strange.

Vanessa sprang down from her rocky hideout and ran toward Lee.

"What's wrong? Is everything OK?" she asked breathlessly.

"Quick. I'll explain as we go." Lee shepherded Vanessa hurriedly onto the tender.

CHAPTER 17

Illegal whaling is an international problem. Despite a ban on commercial whaling since 1986, some countries continue to ignore it or get around it by describing their activities as scientific research.

"One of the tagged whales has turned up," Lee said, waving a small black walkie-talkie type of thing in one hand and using the other to steer the tender. "It's little Ziggy," she added, "one of the young whales."

Her face was flushed with excitement, her eyes shining. They were approaching the trawler, and Mr.

Fox leaned out to pull them in. Vanessa decided to wait until they were on board to ask questions. It was probably not a good time to offer to tie the tender either.

"We'll need Jasper and the team," Lee said to Mr. Fox as they climbed up the steps. "Can you radio them and get them to bring everything? Ziggy is probably two tons by now."

Within minutes, Mr. Fox had started the engines and was on the radio.

Lee turned and, to Vanessa's surprise, took both her hands in her own. Lee might touch Vanessa's arm or kiss her on the cheek, but in general she was not a hand-holder. This must be something very big to be having such an effect on Lee.

"Oh, Vanessa, I'm so relieved," she said happily.

Vanessa smiled encouragingly. "Can you tell me now what's going on?"

"You know about the research lab on Brighton Island and the way they use satellite tracking tags on some of the whales so they can monitor migration patterns? Well, in the last month alone, they have lost the signal on four of their tagged whales. They have just disappeared—all humpbacks and all in the same small area."

"Yes," said Vanessa. "You mentioned that whales were going missing. So you think someone is capturing them? Why would anyone do that, Lee?"

"There is a ban on whaling, but some people don't respect it. They hunt them anyway. They kill the baleen whales—the ones without teeth, the filter feeders—humpbacks and grays, for example."

"But why?" Vanessa asked again.

"Money. Big money. Whale meat is a delicacy in some countries, so hunters kill the whales and sell the meat."

Vanessa made a face. She couldn't imagine wanting to eat whale meat.

"But now Ziggy, one we thought was missing, has turned up." Lee waved the thing that looked like a walkie-talkie at her. "This is the whale tracker," she said, showing Vanessa a screen with a blinking red dot. "We've got a signal back now and it's showing that she is really close to a beach, so we think she may have got stranded."

"So the hunters haven't got her after all?" asked Vanessa.

"Apparently not."

"Are we going to help her? Am I going to see

her?" Vanessa asked incredulously.

Lee smiled. "It's great, isn't it? I'm glad you're here." The radio crackled into life beside them.

"Lee," Mr. Fox called, "it's Jasper on the radio."

"But why did you decide to bring me?" Vanessa asked, just as Lee moved away. Obviously she hadn't heard Vanessa's question, but Mr. Fox had.

"Well," he answered, "Mrs. Bouche called to say she had to go unexpectedly to the mainland today and that she was leaving Wayne with Lettie Cuspard in the ice-cream shop. You couldn't be found, so Lee had to come back to get you," Mr. Fox explained. "She couldn't leave you on your own."

Although he said it in a matter-of-fact sort of way, Vanessa felt as if he had just stuck her with a giant needle. Stinging tears sprang to the corners of her eyes, and she turned to look out to sea. Lee hadn't chosen to bring her along. She was only babysitting her!

CHAPTER 18

Dr. C. MacLean Fraser, who was the head of the Zoology Department in the University of British Columbia from 1920 to 1940, said that "until someone gets a lasso around one of these things we will never be able to get much further. It is possible that there are such things."

The sea was much rougher than yesterday, and the trawler rolled heavily from side to side. Vanessa scanned the water, trying to focus on Ziggy, but her thoughts kept going back to the other creature she had seen, the enormous snakelike monster. Had she imagined it? She couldn't have! But now was not the time to be thinking about the weird creature. She had to concentrate on Ziggy.

"On the beach, just around that next headland!" Lee shouted over the noise of the boat and the wind.

As they came into the bay, three pairs of eyes searched the beach. But they could see nothing.

Lee fiddled with the tracking device.

"We're definitely in the right place," she said flatly. "We'll take the tender on to the beach. You call Jasper and tell him to hold off," she said to Mr. Fox as she climbed into the tender. Lee beckoned to Vanessa to get in and then handed her the tracking device while she started the motor. Lee's face was suddenly grim.

They beached the tender and climbed out into the shallows. Lee was wearing diver's boots, unlike Vanessa, who was wearing her runners, which were now soaking wet. But it didn't matter. Ziggy was all that mattered.

"It should be somewhere around here," Lee said, pointing to the far end of the beach.

"It? You mean Ziggy? Here?" Vanessa was

confused. It was obvious to her that there was no whale on this beach.

"No; sorry, Vanessa. I mean the tag itself—the part that's attached to the whale and sends the signal to the tracker that you're holding."

Lee paused and put her hand to her forehead as if she was taking her own temperature.

Vanessa waited.

"The tag that Dr. Mitchell uses in his research is bullet-shaped and silver-colored. It's attached to a claw that embeds into the whale muscle," Lee explained mechanically.

"Oh, you mean the tag has come off!" Vanessa exclaimed, understanding at last. "So that's what we're looking for, rather than the whale herself?"

Lee nodded. They searched for at least twenty minutes before they found it. Vanessa was delighted to be the one to spot it first. It was partly buried in the sand, and she knelt down and began to dig with her hands.

"Wait, Vanessa!" Lee said, running to her side. She looked as if she was about to say something more but stopped herself.

The tag was exactly as Lee had described it:

bullet-shaped and silver. The other end was attached to something that at first glance might have been a flat rock. It was about the size of a textbook, three inches thick, gray on the outside and a dirty white color inside. Vanessa didn't know what to make of it.

Lee crouched down beside Vanessa and stroked it gently with her hand. She had a strange look on her face.

"It's part of Ziggy's dorsal fin," she said sadly.

Vanessa looked in horror at the piece of fin and then at Lee.

"You mean . . . ?" she said uncertainly, struggling to understand.

"She's dead," Lee said gently. "They killed her and cut off the tag. But this time the tag washed up and we got the signal back."

Vanessa covered her face. She pressed the palms of her hands into her eyes and just about managed to turn away as a wave of nausea rose in her throat. She felt Lee's hand on her back.

"I'm so sorry, Vanessa," Lee said over and over.

"Not your fault," Vanessa said through her tears. "You're trying to stop them."

"No, but I shouldn't have let you see this. I

shouldn't have brought you along. That's why I haven't talked to you about it—I didn't want to upset you."

"How do they kill the whales, these illegal hunters?" Vanessa demanded.

Lee didn't reply.

Vanessa rubbed the back of her hand across her eyes and looked at Lee.

"Tell me, Lee. It's horrible, but I want to know." Lee took Vanessa's hand.

"OK," she said gently. She paused, trying to choose her words. "They harpoon them. They shoot giant arrows into the whales, some of which have explosives in the tips." Lee watched Vanessa's face, hating the pain she was inflicting.

"It can take a long time, but when the whale loses enough blood, it dies."

"Why?" wailed Vanessa, though she knew why. Lee had already told her there was big money in whale meat.

"We should go," Lee said. She pointed at the piece of dorsal fin. "Do you want to carry it, Vanessa?"

Vanessa nodded. They walked back along the beach to the tender, Vanessa cradling what was left of Ziggy's fin in her arms.

CHAPTER 19

Over the years, skeptics have tried to attribute sightings of the sea monster to other known animals such as humpback whales, conger eels, elephant seals, and even basking sharks. However, none of these animals fit the eyewitnesses' descriptions.

True to his promise, Ronan finally rang back.

"Ogopogo!" he yelled down the line without any introduction.

Vanessa's heart skipped.

"So Mum did have a file," she whispered as loudly

as she could. "Open it. Read the first line to me."

"Why are you whispering, Vanessa?"

"Don't want to wake Lee. She's in the room next door and it's two in the morning here."

Ronan chortled. "Sorry, V, I forgot. Bad timing must run in the genes."

"Doesn't matter. Just tell me, Ro."

"He's the most famous water monster in Canada and lives in British Columbia," Ronan read out.

"Fantastic. And the sightings? Where has he been seen? In the sea along the west coast?" asked Vanessa.

"No. This monster lives in a big lake—Lake Okanagan." Vanessa was puzzled. A lake?

"Is Lake Okanagan on one of the gulf islands then?" she said.

Ronan gave a loud, unpleasant snort of laughter, which seemed to be amplified by the thousands of miles between them. "You're the one in Canada, aren't you?" he retorted.

"Please, Ro. Just flick through the folder and see what towns are nearby. See if you can find a map."

She could hear him flipping through the pages. She imagined him sitting at the bottom of the stairs at home, the midnight blue carpet under his bare feet, the awful striped wallpaper in the hall that they had all wanted to change for years, but hadn't, and probably never would now.

"It's a large deep lake in the Okanagan Valley," Ronan read. "Oh, here we go. It's 240 miles east of Vancouver, a five-hour drive if you take the—"

"But that's nowhere near the coast at all."

"Wait, there's a second file for Canada," Ronan said eagerly. "The Sasquatch—a hairy beast that lives in the mountains!"

"Oh, I know about him," Vanessa said dully. "OK, thanks for trying, Ro."

"That's it?" Ronan said. "You're not going to tell me what this is all about?"

Vanessa bit her lower lip. What should she say?

"What exactly are those files of Mum's, Vanessa?"

"You know what they are, Ronan. They're Mum's research into cryptids all over the world. Her monster stories, Luke used to call them. Remember?"

"But they were bedtime stories, Vanessa, weren't they? Just stories she made up?" Ronan sounded puzzled.

Vanessa felt a sudden wave of sadness wash over her. She missed her mum so much—her stories, the wonderful big bear hugs she gave, the frown she wore when she was concentrating, her infectious laugh, and the way she used to rub Vanessa's feet when they watched TV together. She couldn't say anything for a moment.

"Vanessa?" Ronan said when she didn't answer.

There was a sudden kerfuffle at Ronan's end, people talking in the background, and then she heard her dad's voice booming down the line.

"Oh, Nessa, how great to hear from you! You've been away far too long."

Vanessa laughed.

"It's only been a few days, Dad."

"Well, the house just isn't the same without you, love." She could hear the warmth in his voice and pictured him beaming into the phone.

"Tell Lee that I've emailed her that information she wanted—just some legal stuff she asked me about," he explained. "That was a bit tough for you yesterday, Vanessa," her father added.

Vanessa froze.

"Finding the whale fin on the beach. Lee was upset that she'd brought you along."

Vanessa breathed a sigh of relief. Of course he

couldn't have known about the cryptid. Nobody did. Only her.

"It's fine, Dad, honestly," Vanessa said. "I've told Lee not to worry. I'm not a baby, you know."

"Good girl. That's the spirit. That Wayne character behaving himself?" her father added sternly.

Lee must have told her dad about Wayne and the pinching. She felt embarrassed now. What a fuss she had made!

"He's no problem, Dad, honestly. He's a year younger than Ronan—a baby, really."

A baby monster, she felt like adding.

CHAPTER 20

In the 1930s Archie Wills, the editor of the *Victoria Times*, ran a competition to name the creature. The name *Cadborosaurus* was picked because the early sightings were in Cadboro Bay and the Greek root "saurus" means lizard or reptile. After that the monster became known affectionately as Caddy.

It was another beautifully clear day and the sun streamed through Vanessa's bedroom curtains, but when she woke up she felt far from happy. It was Tuesday already. They would be leaving this weekend and she still knew nothing at all about the cryptid she had seen.

After talking to Ronan and her father, Vanessa had fallen back to sleep. She'd had the most vivid dreams about Ziggy—that they had found her on the beach and helped her back into the sea. Ziggy had even thanked her.

Now she had to face the fact again that Ziggy was dead. Vanessa turned onto her side, and her eye was caught by a note propped up against the lamp on her bedside table.

You were exhausted. Decided not to wake you. Back at usual time. Take it easy today. Love, Lee.

Vanessa leaned over the side of the bed, opened her backpack, and took out Toddy. She held the head against her chest.

"They murdered Ziggy," Vanessa whispered. "It makes me sick to think about it."

Well, don't, then, the shrunken head seemed to murmur.

"I can't stop thinking, can I?" Vanessa said impatiently. "More like *they* have to be stopped."

And you think you can do that, do you?

"Yes. No. I don't know, Toddy," she said crossly,

stuffing him under her pillow. "I can see you're going to be no help at all today."

It was nearly half past ten by the time Vanessa finally came down to breakfast. She planned to grab some of the fruit that was always in a bowl on the kitchen table and go off alone to the beach, but it was not to be.

"Good morning, Vanessa. I hope you had a refreshing sleep. I hear you had a very tough day yesterday," Frankie called out as Vanessa picked an apple out of the fruit bowl. She grimaced in sympathy and Vanessa's heart sank. Why did Lee have to tell Frankie Bouche? Now she wouldn't stop talking about it all day.

But Vanessa was wrong. Without another word, Mrs. Bouche produced toast, two fried eggs, and a glass of orange juice and then disappeared into the pantry. Vanessa could see the top of her mousy brown hair as she arranged the shelves. There were enough tins in there to feed an entire regiment of Canadian Mounties, rather than just a couple of guests, Vanessa reckoned.

She couldn't help sighing heavily when Wayne slipped into the chair beside her. She had assumed that by now he'd have eaten his breakfast and be gone somewhere. Anywhere.

"I want my eggs like that," Wayne said loudly.

Frankie shot out of the pantry. The look of pleasure on her face pained Vanessa.

"Are you still hungry, my poor pet?" said Frankie, ruffling her son's hair affectionately.

So this was Wayne's second breakfast.

"Of course you are," Frankie went on proudly. "You're a growing boy."

Greedy pig, Vanessa thought, keeping her head down and eating steadily.

When she lifted her head to take a sip of orange juice she spotted a piece of paper in Wayne's hand. He caught her eye and grinned. Then he ran his hand repeatedly over it, smoothing out the creases. What was he up to? Well, she wouldn't give the little monster the satisfaction of looking at it.

"That's a really good drawing, Wayne," his mother said, putting down his breakfast plate and peering at the page.

Vanessa looked up despite herself. She let out a gasp at what she saw.

"Yes. It is very good, isn't it?" Frankie said,

assuming Vanessa's gasp was one of admiration. "I never knew you were so talented at drawing, Pickles."

Vanessa stared at the page in disbelief. It was her drawing, the one of the cryptid. The heat began in her neck and she felt it spread across her face.

Vanessa bit her lip hard. He must have fished it out from between the rocks.

"It certainly does look just like Caddy. Although I have to say I've never actually seen it myself."

Vanessa stared up at Frankie, searching her face for signs of humor. Perhaps she was making a joke?

"Caddy?" Vanessa echoed. A thousand butterflies began to flutter in her chest.

"Wayne's father, Nigel—he saw Caddy once," Frankie explained, "and he described him just like this—the coils, the funny head. Although I think he also said that Caddy had a kind of hairy ridge along the back of its head and neck too."

She picked up the page and looked closely at the drawing.

"Did you forget that part, Wayne?"

Wayne was grinning too hard at Vanessa to answer his mother.

"Caddy?" Vanessa repeated lamely.

"*Cadborosaurus willsi*," Wayne said, leaning back in his chair. He was enjoying every moment of Vanessa's torment.

Vanessa opened her mouth to speak, but Wayne folded up the drawing, pushed his chair back noisily and disappeared with a cheery wave.

Vanessa finally found her voice. "Cad-what?" she said too loudly.

Frankie looked startled for a second and then her face cleared.

"Oh, you wouldn't have heard of it, dear," she said. "It's just our local sea monster." She gave a little laugh.

Vanessa dropped her fork and it clanked noisily onto the table, but she barely registered it. Here she was being handed really important information on a plate and she couldn't even take in the name.

"What's it called again? The long name that Wayne used," she said urgently.

She could see that Mrs. Bouche was looking at her strangely.

"I think it's Cadiss or Cadissorus—something like that. I'm not great with names, honey. Ask Wayne— he'll tell you lots more about it."

Tell her? It would be like getting blood from a

stone, Vanessa knew. Wayne would make her beg for every morsel of information. Hadn't he just deliberately cleared off as soon as he saw she wanted to talk to him?

Vanessa took her plate to the sink, rinsed off the eggy remains, and put it in the dishwasher.

"I think I'll go and read for a bit," Vanessa said. She needed to go to her room to think.

"I'm almost certain that there's some guy, some professor," Frankie said thoughtfully. "I can't think of his name now. He's up near Tankard's place. He's retired here to write a book about Caddy, I heard."

"Oh my God, that's incredible, Frankie," Vanessa said, clapping her hands together, unable to hide her excitement.

Frankie smiled warmly at Vanessa, delighted at her interest.

"Like Ireland, we've got our very own Loch Ness Monster here. Caddy's not world famous, perhaps, but lots of people here have seen it all the same."

Funny how people always mixed up Ireland and Scotland, Vanessa thought. A bit like the way people confused the US and Canada back home.

She hugged Frankie suddenly—surprising them both.

"Thanks," said Vanessa.

"For what, honey?"

For Caddy, for giving me a lead, for proving I'm not mad, she wanted to say.

"For breakfast," she replied.

CHAPTER 21

In 1994 two scientists proposed that Caddy be recognized as a "new species representative of an unnamed subcategory of reptilian" and that *Cadborosaurus willsi* would be its proper scientific name.

Wayne made himself scarce for the rest of the morning. When he didn't turn up for lunch, Frankie began to display little signs of distress. Her eyes darted to the kitchen window every few seconds.

"I think I'll give Lettie a call and see if Wayne is there," she said finally.

Vanessa heard Frankie on the phone in the hallway. She couldn't make out the words, but the fact that Frankie was laughing was surely a good sign.

"Wayne's at Lettie's all right. He's helping her in the shop and forgot the time. He'll be home later."

Vanessa lowered her eyes to her sandwich and hid her smile by taking a large bite.

"Another glass of milk, honey?" Frankie offered.

Vanessa shook her head. She stood up to take her plate over to the dishwasher, but Mrs. Bouche intercepted her.

"You are such a helpful girl. I'm sure your mom must be very proud of you."

Frankie was being kind. She clearly didn't know that Vanessa's mum had died, but the words were painful all the same. Vanessa swallowed, trying to compose herself before she spoke.

"What are you doing with yourself today then?" Frankie continued.

"Is there a bike I could borrow to go to the village?" Vanessa asked.

An inspired thought had struck her out of the blue: She needed to get away from the guesthouse and see if she could find out more about Caddy and this professor.

"You could borrow Wayne's," Mrs. Bouche suggested. "I don't think he took it when he went out to the village. It's the red and silver one in the shed. I'm sure he wouldn't mind."

Vanessa seriously doubted that, but she took it anyway. There was no need to ask directions. It was a matter of following the road from the guesthouse until it stopped. It took about fifteen minutes to get to Jo-Jo's, and Vanessa really enjoyed the ride.

The hand-painted sign had carved letters in pink and white, and the letters were topped with a swirl of cream, nuts, and marshmallows. There was a giant spoon sticking out of the top. Someone had gone to a lot of trouble to make it.

Vanessa leaned the bike against the wall. She had forgotten to ask about a lock, but looking around, she felt sure it would be safe. Even if someone did steal it, the only way to get it off the island was by private boat, as the ferry was only twice a week. And if you had a private boat, it was highly unlikely you would want a kid's secondhand bike.

Vanessa looked around the sleepy little village. A few cars were parked, but the road was empty, not a living soul in sight. What must it be like on

Duquette Island in the heart of winter? No buses, no taxis, no cinema, no playground. Vanessa shuddered slightly. She imagined the roads covered in snow, the trees a ghostly white. It would be beautiful, but so quiet and so very lonely. Maybe Wayne was to be pitied just a little.

CHAPTER 22

The sea creature known as Caddy has repeatedly been compared to a giant reptile in appearance but also has mammalian features such as hind flippers.

Vanessa pushed against the door of Jo-Jo's, half-expecting it to be locked, as there was nobody inside, but it swung open. She went in, delighted by the bright, cheerful feel of the place. It smelled sweet.

Vanessa looked around. No sign of Wayne. There was a long bar counter with stools and a large display freezer with lots of containers full of ice cream. Vanessa looked at the delicious swirls of color and read their exotic names.

A young woman came out from the back wearing an apron covered in angels.

"Welcome, welcome," she said, spreading her hands out, like a TV preacher welcoming her to church. She had clear blue eyes, and her glossy black hair was smoothed back into a ponytail.

"What can I get you on this beautiful day?" she said, smiling at Vanessa.

Vanessa chose praline brittle in a paper cup rather than a cone and said yes to the hot fudge. Then they chatted. Vanessa was asked about where she was staying and where she was from.

"Oh, Ireland—I've always dreamed of visiting it, so green and beautiful!" the lady behind the counter exclaimed.

"Yes. But it's no greener than here, and your mountains and forests are much more dramatic," Vanessa replied. "And you have such great stories too. I just heard about your sea monster—Caddy."

"Caddy?" said the ice-cream lady, looking puzzled.

"Like Scotland has Nessie—doesn't Canada

have Caddy?" Vanessa persisted, trying to hide her disappointment.

"Oh, you mean Ogopogo. Yeah, sure. He's real famous, like Nessie. But he's a long way off. I grew up in Vernon, a town near the lake, so I know the stories well."

The woman took her cloth and cleaned the full length of the already spotless counter.

"When did you move to the island?" Vanessa asked, thinking that if this woman was a newcomer, that might explain how she'd never heard of Caddy.

"Joe and I moved here about a year ago. He's an artist, and we used to live in the city but decided to move here—slow the pace a little. So he paints and I grow organic vegetables for Givney's store year-round and run this place in the summer." She wrinkled her nose and gave a little laugh. "To be honest, I much prefer ice cream to digging in the dirt." She looked around the shop anxiously. "Did OK last season. Hope this one is better, though."

"It's really nice," Vanessa said with feeling. "I'll bring Lee next time, she loves ice cream. I'm Vanessa, by the way."

"Lettie Cuspard," the woman replied, putting out her hand to shake Vanessa's across the counter.

"Ahhh," Vanessa said with a big grin, "Wayne is a friend of yours, I think."

Lettie gave a hoot of laughter. "Quite a character, Wayne. He was here earlier and he sure does love my ice cream." Then she lowered her voice confidentially as if they were in the middle of a crowd. "To be honest, I think he's found it hard since his daddy left."

Vanessa stopped eating and stared at her. "He left?"

"A few years ago, before we came here. He upped and left overnight. Left a note, that's all."

"How dreadful!" Vanessa said, feeling sorry for Frankie. She even felt a bit sorry for Wayne. Thank goodness she hadn't asked about the photographs of him.

"It's not easy to bring up a child by yourself," Lettie said, busying herself at the sink, without looking up.

Vanessa nodded.

Lettie put out more paper cups and napkins on the counter, although there were plenty there already.

Vanessa looked out of the window, feeling confused and guilty. She didn't like Wayne, but his dad walking out was really tough. It also might explain why Frankie spoiled him.

Vanessa sat up suddenly, her brain registering a familiar-looking man walking on the opposite side of the street. It was the man from the ferry! But he wasn't wearing his yellow raincoat this time, and he certainly looked a lot healthier.

"Who's that, Lettie?" Vanessa asked quickly, nodding her head at him rather than pointing, in case he happened to look over.

"That's Tom Tankard," Lettie said with a look of surprise on her face. "That's very unusual. He rarely comes to town."

"He looks a lot better today," Vanessa said. "He was on the ferry the day we arrived. He looked so unwell, and I felt bad because I nearly knocked him down on the deck."

Lettie's eyes bulged.

"Can't have been Tom Tankard then. He doesn't leave his house often, and the island—never," she said firmly, turning away.

"Really?" Vanessa said faintly.

"Not been the same since his brother's accident. I don't really know him, of course, but they say that he turned a bit strange after that. Unpredictable, if you know what I mean."

Vanessa had no idea what Lettie meant. But the name Tom Tankard rang another bell in her head.

"Frankie was telling me about some scientist," she said brightly. "He lives up near Tom Tankard's, and she says that he has retired here to write a book."

"A scientist, is he? I knew he was a professor and worked at the university in Vancouver all right. He's taken Blackwell's old cottage up beside Tankard's."

Vanessa fished for information: "That's on the road beyond the guesthouse, isn't it?"

"Yes," said Lettie. "The professor lives right at the end of Salem's Lane. And he's dark chocolate and orange." She grinned broadly.

"Sorry?" Vanessa said, thinking she had misheard Lettie.

"I think of people by their ice cream choices," Lettie explained a little shyly. "When you walked in I guessed you were a praline brittle." Lettie appeared quite serious now. "But some days I imagine you're more lemon sherbet." Vanessa laughed but was slightly taken aback all the same. How on earth had Lettie known that lemon sherbet was her other favorite ice cream?

Lettie gave Vanessa a long, hard look.

"I don't think you should go anywhere near Tom Tankard's place, Vanessa," she said seriously. "He likes to be left alone. Rumor has it that he threatened the mayor with a shotgun once."

"What flavor is he, then?" Vanessa said lightly.

She could hardly give a promise not to go near Tom Tankard when she was certainly going to visit the professor who lived right next door.

Lettie didn't answer. She busied herself behind the counter for a minute before offering Vanessa a free refill.

"No, honestly, I'd better just pay and head back to the guesthouse, thanks."

"That'll be a loonie then," Lettie said moving to the cash register.

"Sorry?" Vanessa thought she had misheard again.

"A loonie," Lettie repeated. "A dollar, honey," she explained when Vanessa gave her a blank look.

Vanessa held out a dollar coin.

"Our dollars in Canada are called loonies because there's a picture of a loon on them," she explained pointing to the bird on the coin. "The two dollars are called toonies."

Vanessa laughed. "That's brilliant. We've got

euros at home. It doesn't sound half as good, does it?"

Vanessa paid and left, promising to return with Lee before they left the island. It wasn't until she was freewheeling down the hilly section, with the wind blowing through her hair and chilling her teeth, that she remembered the question she should have asked Lettie—the professor's name! It would be so much easier to introduce herself if she knew his name.

So much for her great detective work! It appeared that "dark chocolate and orange" was the entire sum of her knowledge of the professor so far.

CHAPTER 23

Author Hubert Evans was interviewed for an article in the *Rain-coast Chronicle* in 1994. He confessed to witnessing Caddy with several others years previously, although he was reluctant to admit it. He said the head was "very much like a horse's in general shape, with eye bumps, nostrils and something in the way of ears or horns. . . . It just put the hair up on the back of your neck."

Vanessa approached the cottage at the end of Salem's Lane, unsure what to do now that she had found it. She looked around at the long grass and the overgrown flowerbeds. It didn't look as if the professor enjoyed gardening much.

The house itself was very sweet, and the front door was being painted—half of it was a horrible mustard color and the other a bright green.

As Vanessa stood there, partially hidden by shrubs, the door opened. A man with woolly gray hair and a thick gray beard stepped out with a paint pot in one hand and a brush in the other. Then he stood back to look at the door.

It was now or never, Vanessa thought. She might not get another chance to meet him. If she didn't introduce herself now, she'd never learn about Caddy.

Vanessa stepped out of the shadows and approached the gate.

"Hello," she began. But she stopped suddenly, horrified by her own pushiness. Her father would kill her if he knew she was introducing herself to strange men.

She should probably just turn and walk away. Before she could make a decision, though, she heard him call out.

"No, don't go, please," he said in a friendly voice. "Your timing is perfect. Divine intervention, I'm guessing," he said dramatically. "And now that you're here, I need your advice."

Vanessa smiled shyly. She liked his voice. He was friendly and his manner was easy.

"Just tell me what you think of the color," he called out, waving the paintbrush in his hand.

Vanessa walked up the path and stood in front of the door.

"I'm guessing the hideous mustard color is old and the green new?" she said in an amused voice. "Kelly green. It's brave. I like it. Most people go for just the usual black or blue or red. . . ."

Vanessa's voice trailed off as she ran out of steam. Where did she go from here?

The man laughed.

"That's exactly what I wanted to hear. My wife always claimed that I was color-blind. Now she's passed away I have to rely on my own judgment, which ain't easy sometimes."

He put down the paint pot and offered his hand to Vanessa.

"Jack Noire. Delighted to meet you," he said warmly. There was the slightest hint of an accent that Vanessa couldn't place. Something other than Canadian.

"Vanessa Day. Pleased to meet you too," she replied.

Jack Noire had a weather-beaten face that crinkled when he smiled, like a well-worn leather handbag. He wore a beige T-shirt with paint streaks all over it and long khaki shorts. His feet were bare.

"Think you could do me a favor?" he asked. "Could you check out the color for the sitting room too? I'm not really sure about the one I've picked."

Go into his house? Oh, God! Vanessa felt a sudden rush of adrenaline. Her father and Lee would freak out.

She stared at the professor, wanting desperately to trust her instincts. It was the perfect opportunity, and if she didn't take it, how would she ever find out about Caddy? Wayne was certainly not going to tell her.

Vanessa followed him in through the front door. The hallway wasn't very long and he disappeared almost immediately. Walking slowly to the end of the hall, Vanessa peered into the room. The center of it was filled with furniture. A huge desk, leather armchairs, sofas, chests of drawers, and an assortment of lamps and books were all piled on top of each other.

"A bit of a mess at the moment, I'm afraid, but as

you see, I've got the painting bug. Now tell me what you think. Honestly."

Vanessa looked around. The walls were bright yellow.

"Lemon sherbet," Vanessa exclaimed with a laugh.

"Very fresh. One of my favorite colors and my favorite flavors." For a second, Vanessa was tempted to mention Lettie Cuspard's dark chocolate and orange opinion of him, but she stopped herself in time.

Jack Noire smiled. He was clearly unbothered that she had arrived without invitation at his door and hadn't yet explained her reason for calling.

"Now, this color is for the sitting room but I do think it's a bit too strong," he said, pointing to another pot of paint. It was wine-colored.

Vanessa caught his eye and decided to be direct.

"A bit dark and gloomy, I think. If you want to stay in the reds, something lighter, terracotta maybe, would be nicer."

The professor looked pleased.

"You could try adding a little white and a touch of the yellow into it and see where it ends up," Vanessa suggested.

"Brilliant. OK, that's the paints picked. Let's find

the kitchen table and the kettle and I'll make us a nice cup of tea. That's what the Irish drink all day, isn't it?"

So he'd spotted her Irish accent. At least he hadn't said Scottish.

"Were you born on Duquette Island?" Vanessa asked politely, although she knew he had retired here only recently.

"No, no. Lived most of my life in Vancouver, but born out on Kuper Island. It's a little one between Vancouver Island and the mainland—a native reservation that belongs to the Penelakut."

"Oh, you're Indian!" Vanessa exclaimed. The professor smiled at her.

"We're actually called First Nations these days, although I still like the term Indian myself."

"Is Kuper Island like Duquette?" Vanessa asked.

"Actually, I only lived at home until I was about ten. Then I was sent to the mainland with lots of other kids from the reservation, to a boarding school. I hated it," he said vehemently.

"Why were you sent away?" Vanessa asked.

"So they could knock the savage out of us," he said, smiling. "Don't worry," he continued with a chuckle, "it didn't work on me."

Mr. Fox's comments about civilization and progress flashed into Vanessa's mind. She was about to ask more about the First Nations, but the professor brought the teapot to the table with two cups.

"Milk or lemon?" he said.

"Milk, please." Vanessa gazed out of the big bay window to the sea. She'd love a house like this someday, right on the edge of the ocean.

"So," said her host, "you've been kind enough to listen to my life story and to help me pick my paints. Now, what can I do for you in return?"

"Well," Vanessa said, leaning forward in her chair, "you're a professor, I hear."

"Retired professor of marine biology—worked in the University of British Columbia for thirty years. But please, call me Jack. You can't help me pick my paint colors and then call me Professor Noire."

"OK," said Vanessa.

"Now ask me," Jack said grinning at her. "I can see you'll burst if you don't."

Vanessa was taken aback. Was she that easily read? She inhaled deeply. "Tell me everything you know about Caddy," she blurted out.

CHAPTER 24

The most famous book about Cadborosaurus was written by scientists Paul LeBlond and Edward Bousfield and was published in 1995. It is called *Cadborosaurus: Survivor from the Deep.*

Vanessa drank her tea and listened as Professor Noire—Jack—spoke.

"I saw Caddy for the first time in Turner Bay in 1964. She just popped up out of the blue beside me while I was fishing with my brother Larry. We used to go out fishing once a week." Jack leaned back in his chair. "After that we went out every day, but I didn't see Caddy again for another twenty years. By that stage I was beginning to think I had imagined the whole thing."

He paused and frowned.

"The only problem with the hallucination theory was the fact that Larry and I had both seen the exact same thing at the same time. How could we both have imagined it? I asked myself. So in the end it seemed more rational to believe that we did see a strange creature in the sea that day."

Vanessa looked at Jack's lined face. It was an honest face. She was dying to ask him to describe the creature, but if she interrupted now, goodness knows what else she would miss.

"Soon after that, I began to go through the old newspapers and magazines to see where Caddy popped up. Larry got bored with the whole thing, but I became obsessed. I couldn't believe the number of witnesses Caddy had. From that point on, I began to collect details of all the sightings."

Jack stopped to pour Vanessa some more tea from the pot. Then he noticed that there was no more milk in the jug and started to get up.

"I drink it black too, thanks," Vanessa said quickly, taking a sip. She didn't care about the tea—she wanted him to sit down and keep talking.

"The reports go back right to the turn of the twentieth century. Most were just ordinary people taken by surprise and reluctant to admit it, but they felt that what they had seen was so extraordinary that they had to tell someone. Over time, other people heard what I was doing and got in touch with me. I got them to describe it and draw a picture if they could."

Vanessa thought of the picture that she'd drawn and that Wayne now had. She wouldn't say anything yet. Plenty of time for her story later.

Jack got up from the table, went over to a huge bookshelf and ran his fingers along the spines, searching for something.

"Found you," he said, plucking out a small paperback book and presenting it with both hands to Vanessa. "You should read this. It's the bible on Caddy."

Vanessa looked at the title. *Cadborosaurus: Survivor from the Deep* by Paul LeBlond and Edward L. Bousfield. She opened it reverently and read the first lines:

This book is about Caddy, British Columbia's sea serpent. Although reported by hundreds of eyewitnesses over the past century, this animal remains a "cryptid": a creature whose existence is still in doubt because of insufficient material evidence.

"Oh my God! This is so incredible, Jack. Normally I have to hunt to the ends of the earth to find out about a cryptid, and here you are, just handing me a whole book about Caddy. Do you know these people who wrote it—Paul LeBlond and Edward Bousfield?" She read the names from the cover.

"Oh, yes indeed. I've met them both, and I've met Heulvemann too. He's the father of cryptozoology."

"I can't believe it," Vanessa said dramatically. "I'm standing here talking to a real cryptozoologist."

"And I can't believe I've met a kid who knows what a cryptozoologist is!" Jack laughed. "How come?"

"It's my mum," Vanessa said, stumbling over her words. "She is . . . she was . . . she was fascinated by cryptids and kept files on them—the Loch Ness Monster, the Chupacabra, Ogopogo. . . ."

"And Caddy?" Jack added.

"No, not Caddy. Mind you, it was only Ronan

checking for me, so he could have missed it."

Jack didn't ask who Ronan was or pepper her with questions like most people would. Instead he took a drink of his tea and waited for her to explain.

"Can I borrow the book, please? Just for a few days?" said Vanessa.

"Of course. I'm sorry I can't give it to you to keep—it's my only copy and it's out of print now."

"I promise I won't lose it. I won't let it out of my sight even for a moment," Vanessa said, clutching the book to her chest. "I'd better go, or Lee will be worried," she said then, forgetting that she hadn't explained who Lee was or what they were doing on the island. "Can I come again?"

She stood up from the table.

"Absolutely, Vanessa," said Jack. "You've still got to pick the paint color for the hall."

CHAPTER 25

Although Caddy is only rarely seen at the surface, all indications are that it is an air-breather. Several observers have described nostrils at the snout end of the head and some have described "steam" or "jet" emissions from them.

—Cadborosaurus: Survivor from the Deep

Lee was sitting at the kitchen table with Frankie when Vanessa arrived back. There was a big pot of coffee between them, which was almost empty. Lee jumped up when she saw Vanessa and hugged her without saying a word.

When she had arrived back, Lee had been surprised to find that Vanessa was not in the guesthouse or on the beach. At first she had tried not to let herself worry, but distant ripples—the memory of Vanessa's disappearance in Scotland not so long ago—began to gather momentum in Lee's head. An hour drinking coffee with Mrs. Bouche hadn't soothed her nerves either.

She's just biked to the village, Lee had reminded herself. *She needed to get away from Wayne for a bit, that's all.*

But another part of Lee wondered why Vanessa had been gone so long.

Vanessa knew immediately from Lee's face that she had been worried, and she was annoyed with herself. How would she explain about going into Jack Noire's cottage now? What an idiot she was!

"Sorry. I got talking to a professor," Vanessa said brightly, hoping that the "professor" bit might distract Lee. She made it sound as if she had just met him in town.

"Oh, Lee, I'd forgotten all about him," Mrs. Bouche exclaimed. "So you found him, Vanessa. Well done, you!" She patted Vanessa enthusiastically on the shoulder.

For some reason that Vanessa couldn't quite understand herself, she wanted to keep Caddy a secret from Lee—just for the moment. She would tell her soon, but there was a lot of stuff to read and digest first. Besides, Lee had the whales to worry about. The image of Ziggy's sliced dorsal fin hit her suddenly. How could she have forgotten?

Lee looked from Frankie to Vanessa and back again, waiting for further explanation.

"He's a professor of . . ." Mrs. Bouche stopped. She had no idea of what.

"Marine biology," Vanessa said quickly. "He's retired now, but he worked for thirty years in the University of British Columbia. You know, the one in Vancouver, Lee. It sounded like an amazing place."

Vanessa was beginning to babble and she knew that Lee would spot it soon. She just had to keep the conversation away from cryptids. Otherwise Mrs. Bouche would bring up Caddy sooner or later.

"The professor was really interesting. He knew so much about whales," Vanessa said, meeting Lee's eyes and hoping the mention of whales would throw her on to a different track.

Lee looked slightly stunned but said nothing.

"I'm starving," Vanessa said heartily. "Did I miss dinner, Frankie? I'm really sorry."

Vanessa felt her guilt as a lead weight in her stomach. She wasn't the tiniest bit hungry. All she wanted was to go to her bedroom and read the Cadborosaurus book. She had to understand what she had seen first; then she would tell Lee.

"Is Wayne back yet?" Vanessa persisted.

Surely the mention of the precious one would finally change the subject?

"He's just back too," said Frankie cheerfully. "I'm surprised you two didn't bump into each other in town."

Lee gave Vanessa a questioning look. Was it so obvious that she was hiding something?

"I'll get the dinner on the table," said Frankie, heaving herself up and going to a large pot sitting on the stove. She hummed a tune under her breath, unaware of the tension in the room.

Lee sidled up to Vanessa.

"You didn't discuss Ziggy with the professor, did you, Vanessa?" she said quietly.

"Absolutely not, Lee!" Vanessa said with conviction. "Nothing at all about Ziggy or the humpbacks, I promise." At least on that score she was telling Lee the absolute truth.

CHAPTER 26

On 5 January 1934 Murray Jackson, Billy Alexander, and three friends saw a creature with a 4-foot long neck and a cowlike head with horns or ears. It was reported in the *Vancouver Sun* later that week.

That evening, Vanessa propped Toddy up against her pillow and flicked through the book. Her eye was caught by a silly rhyme about Caddy, which she read out loud to herself.

British Columbians! Lift up a chorus!
To greet the arrival of Cadborosaurus!
He may have been here quite a long time before us,
But he's shy and don't stay round too long, so's to bore us.
Cadborosaurus! Cadborosaurus!
Come up and see us again, you old war 'oss!

"See, Toddy, Caddy is famous in this part of the world." Vanessa let the book drop onto her lap and leaned back on the bed. "Lee would love that—she loves rhymes and limericks."

She felt guilty keeping Caddy a secret. So why not tell Lee? After all, Lee had shared Vanessa's adventure with Nessie.

Vanessa sighed. Her thoughts returned to their walk along the beach after dinner. She just hadn't found the right moment to mention Caddy. Lee had done most of the talking. She seemed to want to talk about the whales, and Vanessa had been very happy to listen. They had not discovered anything new about the whale hunters, Lee had said, but they had gotten great recordings of the whales' song.

"It's amazing, Vanessa. The male humpbacks in the same area sing the same song. So the North Pacific males sing something different from the southern hemisphere males. But the next year when they migrate back up from Hawaii, the song has evolved into something new."

It was getting dark by the time they came in.

"Oh, I forgot to tell you the most important thing, though," Lee said as they climbed the stairs. "Dr. Mitchell said it would be OK for you to visit the research center with me on Friday."

Vanessa had been thrilled. Just two days away—she couldn't wait!

She put down her book now and picked up Toddy.

"Any ideas about the illegal whale hunting?" Vanessa asked him.

Nothing.

"I wonder how Lee is going to track them down."

Nothing.

Vanessa smoothed the long hair off the face of the shrunken head, put it back on the pillow, and said sternly, "OK, if you're not prepared to talk, then you can listen and learn."

Vanessa read the first chapter of the book to Toddy. She did it quietly, listening all the time for sounds of people on the stairs, just in case. It was interesting stuff about cryptozoology and the definitions, but Vanessa really wanted to know about Caddy. She flicked ahead, skipping through the pictures of native petroglyphs made by the Indian tribes, who spoke of a sea serpent in the waters.

She stopped at a picture of a man in a suit and tie with the words "Caddy's 'godfather,' Archie Wills" underneath. She read on.

The first mention of the name "Cadborosaurus" appeared on 11 October 1933. Several suggestions for names for the monster had been received by the Victoria Daily Times, *one of which is "Cadborosaurus," which can be shortened to "Caddy," in honor of Cadboro Bay, where the creature was first sighted.*

Vanessa's eyes stopped on a picture of Caddy. It was a postcard from 1933, drawn by Charles Eagles. Beneath it she read, "Body approximately twenty feet, tail thirty feet, head and neck ten feet. Total length sixty feet."

While she couldn't really say much about the length of the creature she'd seen, the head certainly looked similar.

She wriggled with suppressed excitement. She read on.

"Your modern man would rather disbelieve something than believe it," Archie Wills wrote. "He likes to think he is cynical and hard-boiled, whereas he is the most credulous creature ever made. When he can't understand a thing like astronomy, or relativity, or finance, he believes anything you care to tell him, if you tell him with sufficient scientific or financial trimmings. But the trouble is he can understand a sea serpent. He can visualize it. Therefore he disbelieves it. His disbelief flatters his vanity, makes him think he is a superior fellow. Well, it doesn't make him a superior fellow. Any fool can disbelieve in sea serpents."

"That's almost exactly what my mum used to say to me, Toddy. She said that some scientists believe that science is truth, whereas science sometimes clouds the truth and hides the obvious."

Vanessa shut the book with a snap. She wouldn't allow herself to read the whole thing in one go. That would be gorging herself. She would take it bit by bit, digest it, and think about it.

"What do you think I should do? I mean, should I

discuss it with Lee?" Vanessa mused. "Or find out as much as I can first?"

The sightless eyes stared at her.

"Maybe you're right. Keep silent for the moment. Knowledge is power, or something like that. Caesar said so."

Vanessa turned off her lamp and lay down.

"Night, Toddy," she murmured as she tucked him under her pillow. She always hid him when she was going to sleep in case someone came into her room.

It was Sir Francis Bacon who said that, actually.

It was the gentlest of whispers that tickled her inner ear, but Vanessa heard it and laughed.

She closed her eyes. "You're such a know-it-all!" she replied.

CHAPTER 27

In September 1963 the carcass of a sea creature was found near Oak Harbor, Whidbey Island. Although it appeared to have a head that resembled a horse, Mr. Welander of Fisheries is said to have thought it was a basking shark.

"Can I borrow the bike again, please, Frankie?" Vanessa asked politely the next morning after breakfast.

Mrs. Bouche frowned. "I think you know why that's impossible, Vanessa," she said sternly. "Wayne was really very upset last night."

"I only borrowed it for a few hours, Frankie," Vanessa said defensively. "I'm sorry I was late back."

"New tires will have to be sent from the mainland," Frankie said, as if she hadn't heard her. "It could take weeks, not to mention the money involved."

Vanessa stared at Mrs. Bouche, shocked to see how upset she was.

"It was very, very careless of you," Frankie said crossly. "I think you should apologize to Wayne. He was so generous, lending it to you in the first place."

Fighting an internal battle between her rising indignation and the worry that she had somehow damaged the bike without realizing it, Vanessa stared wildly at Mrs. Bouche. She didn't point out that it was Frankie who had done the lending. Wayne wouldn't have let her anywhere near his bike.

"I'm sorry, Frankie," she said eventually. "I really don't know what you mean. I rode it back from Jack Noire's and it was fine."

"Well, I'm not sure how two punctured tires can be called 'fine,' Vanessa. I checked the bike myself this morning when Wayne told me, and it's true."

"But that's terrible," Vanessa said hotly. "Of course I'll find Wayne and sort it out with him." She mumbled something under her breath and then finished with the words "pay for it."

Mrs. Bouche looked up and gave her a small, grateful smile.

"Thank you, Vanessa. It was the fact that you said nothing that bothered Wayne, more so than the money. But we do appreciate your offering to pay."

Vanessa nodded silently. She would make Wayne pay for this all right. She felt a cold fury growing in her chest and she pursed her lips for fear of what she might say. She excused herself and then flung herself out the back door into the yard.

"I'm going to kill him," she whispered over and over as she searched for Wayne, slamming the doors of the various outhouses and sheds as she went.

Vanessa could see that Mrs. Bouche was staring out of the kitchen window at her. She looked really sad and that made Vanessa even more furious. Why had Wayne done it? Was it just spite—or did he have a screw loose?

Vanessa found the bike sitting against the outside wall of the utility room. Kneeling down, she inspected the tires. It was obvious to her that they weren't just punctured. They had been slashed with a knife.

She felt another wave of intense fury wash over her, and she kicked the wheel so hard she hurt her foot. Why? Was Wayne trying to get her in trouble? Make things so horrible that she'd want to leave?

Any vestige of pity that Vanessa had felt for Wayne disappeared. He really was dangerous. She'd have to be careful, but she would find a way to get him back.

CHAPTER 28

Vancouver restaurateur Peter Pantages; his wife, Helen; and their friend Chris Altman saw Caddy while they were fishing in English Bay in 1947. Mrs. Pantages said that the animal had a horse's face and three humps, and it swam up and down like a caterpillar.

There was no sign of Wayne on the beach, but Vanessa took a stick to the bushes to make sure he wasn't hiding there. She walked to the very end. On the way back she found that the famous Duquette fresh air was beginning to work its magic, and she felt calmer.

When she found a smooth, flat rock that looked inviting, she decided to sit down for a bit. She stared out at the horizon. The sun warmed her head. It felt nice.

Would she ever see Caddy again? she wondered. She imagined his funny head suddenly breaking the surface of the water right in front of her and she smiled to herself. If only! Jack had said that he had to wait twenty years for his second sighting—and she only had three more days left on the island. It was hard to believe that a week ago she had never even heard of *Cadborosaurus willsi*. Vanessa picked up a stone and threw it into the water. Her mum had always said that passion and patience were important traits for a cryptozoologist. Well, she certainly had the passion. Now all she had to do was work on the patience.

Vanessa's eyes picked out a boat in the distance. It looked as if it was coming into the next bay. Was it Mr. Fox's? Was Wayne with him? Maybe she should go and have a look.

Vanessa took her time. As she rounded the corner that led to the next bay, she stopped abruptly. Mr. Fox was on the beach talking to a man that she didn't recognize. Vanessa ducked behind a rock. She was sure they hadn't seen her, as they were deep in conversation. There was something in Mr. Fox's hand, but she would have needed binoculars to make it out properly.

Then she had a brainwave. She opened her backpack, pulled out her camera, lifted it to her eye, and zoomed in. She could see it quite clearly now: It was just like the GPS tracker that Lee had used the day they'd found Ziggy's fin.

Vanessa continued to watch, and then almost through force of habit she pushed down the button and took a photo. Then a few more.

As the men shook hands, something else passed between them. Was it money? Was Mr. Fox selling the tracker to this other man? Why? It had all happened too quickly and Vanessa wasn't sure if she had caught it on camera.

The two men looked around and Vanessa ducked down.

She waited for a while before looking again. By then they were going their separate ways: Mr. Fox to the tender and the other man back up the rocky slope and through the trees.

When they were gone, Vanessa hurried back along the beach as quickly as she could. Who was that other man, and what had they been talking about? And had money actually changed hands, as she'd thought?

Near the bottom of the steps to the guesthouse, Vanessa sat down on a fallen tree trunk and looked at the pictures again. She was disappointed to find that there was nothing really suspicious in the photos. It just looked like two men talking on a beach. If she zoomed in she could make out the whale tracker in Mr. Fox's hand, but that was all. Perhaps it was an innocent meeting and the second man was also working on Brighton Island. So why did it not feel right to her?

She heaved a sigh. Maybe she was letting her imagination run away again. Worse—what if she was actually turning into Wayne? After just a few days in his company, she was already spying on people and sneaking around taking photographs.

CHAPTER 29

I must confess, I believe in sea serpents——perhaps because Caddy's lovable nature intrigues my imagination. I like the idea of this homely monster coming up from the caverns of the deep every so often, just to have a look around and see how we're getting along.

——Canada's Monsters, *Betty Sanders Garner*

Vanessa packed the essentials into her backpack—a bottle of water, Toddy, her camera, and Jack's book—and set out for Salem's Lane. She needed to talk to the professor. It was time to tell him about her sighting.

Maybe she would tell him about Mr. Fox too, see what he made of it.

The occasional car passed Vanessa on the road, and each driver honked and gave her a big wave on the way past. It was a friendly island, yet nobody stopped to offer her a lift.

Even if they did, she wouldn't get in, she decided. Going into Professor Noire's cottage was bad enough, but getting into a stranger's car would be pushing her luck.

She could see the roof of the cottage in the distance and was aware of another house to the left, just before it. It must be Tom Tankard's house, Vanessa guessed. Lettie had said he'd gone a bit strange after his brother's accident. Vanessa wondered fleetingly what type of accident it had been, and as she walked past the front entrance she slowed out of curiosity. She wasn't sure what she was expecting, but the sight of a man in a yellow raincoat walking down the drive stopped her in her tracks. Why was Tom Tankard wearing a coat today? It wasn't a stone-splitter of a day, but it didn't look like rain either.

Without thinking about it, Vanessa pushed open the gate and followed him. There was a curve in the drive, and when she came around the bend she stopped. There was no sign of Tom Tankard anywhere. Had he gone inside?

Too late to turn back now, Toddy whispered from the security of her backpack.

"True," Vanessa said thoughtfully, looking up at the windows in the house and wondering if Tom was watching her.

She walked purposefully up to the front door and knocked. As she waited, she spotted an old-fashioned ship's bell. Maybe she should try that instead. She pulled it gently, and it responded with a loud, unpleasant clanking. Vanessa grabbed the bell to stop the noise.

The door swung open and Tom Tankard stared at her in astonishment. His eyes were clear, and he looked much healthier than he had that day on the boat.

"Oh, I'm sorry," Vanessa said quickly. "I'm looking for Professor Jack Noire's house. They told me in the village that he lived somewhere on Salem's Lane."

Vanessa hoped she didn't sound as nervous as she felt. The man nodded to the right. Still he said nothing.

"Oh, the house next door? Thanks."

Vanessa paused. She'd give it a go, she thought. She'd try to draw him out.

"I'm sorry I came to the door. I've met you before, actually—on the ferry last Saturday, wasn't it?"

The man stared at her, his eyes narrowed.

Vanessa was beginning to feel increasingly uncomfortable. She should just mind her own business in the future. And she would have to talk to Toddy later about his misleading and unhelpful comments.

Vanessa began to back away, apologizing for the intrusion. Unpredictable, Lettie had said. He had threatened the mayor with a shotgun, she'd said. Maybe he had it loaded in the hallway right now.

"Sorry I bothered you. Really, I am. And I'm really sorry about almost knocking you overboard too. I should have spotted you in that bright yellow raincoat, but I didn't."

Just stop talking and go, she scolded herself.

It was as if the man, wound like a spring, was suddenly released. He lunged at her and grabbed her hands. Vanessa screamed and tried to pull away. When she bent down to bite his hands, he suddenly let them go.

"Sorry, sorry," he panted, his eyes wide, his jaw chewing furiously as if he was trying to make the words come. "I'm sorry." He looked about wildly.

Vanessa drew back out of his reach but stood her ground. Although her heart was hammering, she found she wasn't afraid. She had never seen a man look so sad and pathetic.

"What do you mean a yellow raincoat?" he said in a hoarse whisper. "Did you think it was me wearing it?"

"Yes. Wasn't it you? You were on the deck of the ferry. I thought you were seasick."

"Dear God," Tom murmured, leaning against the doorway for support. He looked like a rag doll with its stuffing knocked out.

What on earth was she to do now? Vanessa wondered. Help him to a chair? But she didn't want to go inside.

"Why you?" Tom demanded in a strangled whimper. "Why not me?"

And then to her astonishment he began to sob quietly. Vanessa shifted on her feet. Part of her wanted to run, but the other part wanted to know what he meant.

"Come in," he said through his tears. "We have to talk."

"No," she said suddenly, "I have to go. Lee is expecting me."

She hoped her voice didn't sound as panicky as she felt. Never mind about going into the professor's house—she was certainly not going into Tom Tankard's.

CHAPTER 30

The International Society of Cryptozoology was founded in 1982. Dr. Paul LeBlond, author of *Cadborosaurus: Survivor from the Deep*, is a former director.

Vanessa could feel Tom Tankard's eyes boring into her back as she walked purposefully down the drive and out of the gate. She'd given up on the idea of visiting the professor today. That could wait.

As soon as she was out of sight, she started to run, her heart thumping, her backpack bouncing awkwardly on her back. What had all that been about?

Why did Tom Tankard insist on wearing the silly yellow coat and then get so upset when she mentioned it? Had he been on the boat for some secret reason and was annoyed that she had seen him? It didn't make sense.

Vanessa stumbled slightly as she ran, and pain shot up through her ankle. She collapsed onto a patch of grass at the side of the road, panting heavily. That was all she needed, she thought, massaging her ankle furiously.

Slowly the pain began to ebb away. Her ankle was OK. She'd just have to rest for a bit. Pulling Toddy out of her bag, she cradled the head in her lap and her breathing slowed. She felt calmer. How could his expressionless face manage to look knowing and disdainful at the same time?

"Oh, don't pretend you knew all along that was going to happen," Vanessa said impatiently. "And if you did, you might have warned me. 'Turn back,' 'Use your head'... Anything like that would have been helpful. Instead you say, 'Too late to turn back!'"

Toddy remained silent. Only the birds cackled overhead. By the time Vanessa arrived back to the guesthouse, Lee was coming down the stairs for dinner, so she didn't have time to tell her about the bike. It was, of course, the very first thing that Wayne brought up when they sat at the table. To Vanessa's relief, Lee took it in her stride. No doubt there would be questions later, though.

"That's really unfortunate," Lee said mildly. "We'll get those tires fixed for you, Wayne, don't you worry," she said, patting his hand on the table before turning to Mrs. Bouche.

"Frankie, won't you sit down with us? You're always slaving away in that kitchen for us three and never actually eating."

The chicken casserole that Frankie produced was delicious, and Lee entertained them with stories about killer whales.

"Whaling was a big thing, historically, on this island," Frankie told them. "Once upon a time there was a whaling station on the west coast, over near Carlingford Point. Nothing there now of course. Not many fishermen left either on these islands."

"Why, Frankie?" asked Vanessa.

"Not much of a living for an individual with all these commercial boats scooping up thousands of tons," Frankie explained.

"Yes. And scooping up the seabed without a thought for all that they are destroying," Lee added sternly.

"The Tankard brothers were the last real fishermen on Duquette," Frankie said, shaking her head sadly.

"I spoke to Tom Tankard this afternoon," Vanessa said, trying to sound casual. "What is his brother called?"

Mrs. Bouche's fork stopped midway to her mouth, and she gawped at Vanessa.

"Dead. The other one's dead," Wayne said, with great emphasis on the word dead.

Vanessa stared. She had heard about the accident, but she hadn't actually known for sure that he was dead.

"What was his name?" she asked again, although she wasn't sure why.

"His name was Ray," Frankie replied. "But you say you spoke to Tom this afternoon?"

Frankie's eyebrows shot up into her forehead. It was clear to Vanessa that she didn't believe her.

"His house is up near the professor's and I saw

him in the garden. We had a few words as I passed by," Vanessa explained, kicking herself for having mentioned his name at all.

"That's extraordinary! Tom hasn't spoken to anyone on the island for nearly a year." Frankie paused. "Not since his brother drowned."

All eyes were on Vanessa, who was mortified. They all probably thought she was making the whole thing up now.

"Weird," Wayne said with a sneer. "I wonder why he suddenly started talking to you, Vanessa, when you were just passing."

Vanessa's eyes widened. Had he been following her again? Had he seen her call to Tom Tankard's house?

Wayne smiled lazily and she could almost imagine the forked tongue flicking out through his lips. He really was the closest thing to a human snake she had ever come across.

"I think it was especially hard for Tom," Frankie said with a slow shake of her head, "because Ray was his identical twin. It was like losing part of himself, really. They were inseparable in life and Tom just can't get over his death."

An identical twin? Vanessa's head began to spin.

"Does Tom ever go on the ferry to the mainland, Frankie?" Vanessa said abruptly, remembering what Lettie had said.

"Dear me, no," Frankie said with conviction. "Never." Vanessa felt the prickles on her skin spread like a rash all over her body. She stared at her half-eaten dinner, her appetite gone. Finally she understood Tom's words and why he had been so agitated with her.

It wasn't Tom she had seen on the ferry, but his twin, Ray. And what's more, she had seen him again today in Tom's garden, wearing that yellow coat! Or at least, she had seen his ghost.

Why you? Why not me? Tom had kept saying.

Yes, why indeed, Vanessa thought grimly. Why was she the one to see Ray, rather than his grief-stricken brother?

But there was no explanation, Vanessa knew that. It had happened before. She just saw things.

CHAPTER 31

On 21 July 1998 it was reported in the *Victoria Times Colonist* that the Campbell family, who were out in a boat near Senanus Island in order to spread their dead son's ashes, saw a creature that fitted the description of Caddy. "I'm a believer now," Hugh Campbell claimed afterward.

The next morning, Vanessa woke to a sliver of blue sky and a stream of sunshine through a parting in the curtains, all thoughts of drownings and ghosts dispelled. There was a gentle knock on the door.

"Come in," Vanessa called out, guessing it was Lee. The door handle rattled, but the door remained shut.

"Sorry," Vanessa yelled, getting out of bed to open it. "I forgot I locked it last night." She smiled at Lee. "Don't want Wayne snooping around."

"Good girl," Lee said, giving her a peck on the cheek. "Just wondering what you're planning to do. Thought it might be a good idea if you stayed away from him today."

"I promise you, Lee, I had nothing to do with the bi— " Vanessa began, but Lee cut across her.

"Of course you hadn't, Vanessa," Lee said indignantly. "I never thought you had. I just think, for your own sanity, you need to keep your distance. We go home in two days anyway, so you won't have to put up with him for too much longer."

Two days? They were going home in two days! She had to see Caddy again. And what about the whales?

"What about Ziggy and the other whales? Have you caught anyone yet?" said Vanessa.

"Not yet," Lee admitted glumly. "But all the other tags seem to be moving normally. So maybe it's stopped. I'll be coming back in a few months' time anyway. It will be an ongoing investigation, I imagine."

Ongoing without me, thought Vanessa. It would be so much easier for Lee to be here on her own with no distractions.

"Lucky you," Vanessa said heavily. "I suppose you'll have Mr. Fox again as your captain when you come back?"

Lee looked slightly taken aback. "Possibly. Why do you ask, Vanessa?"

"Oh, nothing. Just wondered if you use other locals too. I saw Mr. Fox talking to a guy on the beach and wondered if he worked on Brighton Island."

Vanessa knew that her explanation didn't make much sense. But Lee wasn't really listening and stood up to go.

"So what's the plan?" Lee asked again.

"Think I'll walk into town and get an ice cream at Jo-Jo's," Vanessa replied. "I can't believe we're going home so soon, Lee."

Lee grinned and prodded Vanessa with her index finger.

"You like it here? Even with Wayne and the fact

that there's nothing other than curly arbutus trees, sea breezes, and fresh air?"

Vanessa laughed. "You're forgetting about those giants in the sea. They are certainly worth being here for."

"Yes. The whales are very special," Lee agreed.

True. But Caddy was even more special, Vanessa mused. If only she could see that giant one more time!

CHAPTER 32

Andy Hillstrand, a fisherman from the TV series *Deadliest Catch*, saw a video taken by Kelly Nash of the elusive Cadborosaurus in Alaska. "Spray came out of its head; it was definitely not a shark. A giant eel may be possible, but eels don't have humps that all move in unison. I've never seen anything like it before," he said.

Vanessa bought a nut-brittle sundae with chopped nuts and hot chocolate sauce and picked a table in the window of Jo-Jo's. She was disappointed to find that Lettie wasn't there. Instead, she was served by a sullen-looking girl who prepared her ice cream without saying a word.

"Will Lettie be in later today?" Vanessa asked in a friendly voice as she sat down.

"No," the girl replied rudely.

So much for the friendly locals, Vanessa thought. No point in asking her about the Tankard twins either.

Looking out into the harbor, Vanessa could see a large fishing trawler tied up to the pier.

"What type of boat is that?" Vanessa asked. "I haven't seen it here before."

The girl looked up, an expression of naked boredom on her face.

"It's a crab boat," she said shortly. And then to Vanessa's surprise she continued. "They're refueling. I've seen them a few times this last month."

Vanessa could see some of the crew members moving about on the deck. With a sudden sense of shock, she recognized one of them. It was the man she had seen on the beach with Mr. Fox, the one she'd thought was a bit suspicious. He was heavyset, with jet-black hair and a thick beard.

"Is it a local boat?" Vanessa called out to the girl behind the counter.

The girl looked up from what she was doing, almost as if she was surprised to find Vanessa still in the shop.

"Not from around here," she said, shutting her mouth in a firm line.

Stop bothering me was written all over the girl's pasty face. Vanessa picked up her backpack. She would take a closer look at the trawler, she decided. See what its name was.

Vanessa didn't bother to say good-bye. *That girl's face could turn your ice cream sour,* she thought.

As Vanessa approached the pier, she started to worry about being seen. But then she remembered that Mr. Fox and the crab man hadn't seen her on the beach that day, so it made no difference.

She worked out a couple of introductory sentences, in case she needed them. Something about the *Deadliest Catch* series on TV, which was all about real life on the crab boats in Canada and Alaska.

There was nobody out on deck by the time she stood at the gangplank, so she rested her hand tentatively on the rail. Could she sneak on board for a quick look? Vanessa waited, listening for voices and hearing none. Then, before she could lose her nerve, she walked up the ramp and onto the boat.

CHAPTER 33

Caddy is extremely agile in the water. Speeds of up to 40 knots have been reported.

Vanessa moved quickly toward the stern. Now that she was on board, she could hear the men working at the bow. She was a little disappointed to find there wasn't much to see, and she was just about to turn around when she noticed some big metal containers. She tried the handle of a small trapdoor in the top of one of them, assuming it wouldn't yield. Yanking it as hard as she could, she was surprised when the lid opened with ease on its well-oiled hinges.

Yuck! Vanessa recoiled at the sight of thousands of huge crabs in water, piled on top of each other. All spikes and legs. She dropped the lid quickly.

The other containers looked the same, but farther along the deck she spotted a much smaller one. Probably more crabs, but maybe she should check it out anyway.

When she opened the lid, a blast of cold air from the refrigerator hit her. This time instead of writhing crabs she was faced with huge slices of bloody meat. Some enormous fish? Tuna? No, it looked thicker than that.

Could it be whale meat? Could it be Ziggy? Vanessa gave a yelp at the thought and dropped the lid. It made a clanking noise and she cursed silently. What if someone came to investigate?

She hid behind a pillar and waited, but nobody came. If it was whale meat in the refrigerator, then these fishermen were the illegal hunters, and Lee needed to know straight away. But would Vanessa be able to find Lee and show her before the boat left the harbor? It was just refueling, the girl in Jo-Jo's had said. No. She would have to get the evidence herself before she left the boat.

At least Vanessa had her camera and could take some photographs. She really didn't want to look again, but she had no choice. She'd do it quickly, for the sake of Ziggy and the others, she decided.

Taking her camera out of her backpack, Vanessa lifted the lid gingerly. She held it open with one hand and tried to hold the camera with the other. She pushed down on the button, but her hands were shaking so much that the camera slipped from her grip and into the refrigerator.

"No!" she cried, as it slithered down beneath the meat.

She snatched it back up, but the strap caught on something. She yanked it again and this time it drew up something metal-looking. It was a bullet-shaped tracking tag just like the one that had been attached to Ziggy's dorsal fin.

"Oh my God!" The words caught in Vanessa's throat. It was one of the research whales. These people really were the hunters—and they were using the research institute's own GPS tracking devices to locate and kill the whales. But how had they gotten the tracker? From Mr. Fox? Was that the transaction she had seen on the beach that day? She must have been right about him after all.

The thought of it brought tears to Vanessa's eyes, but there was no time to cry now. She had to take the photos. She would need them to back up her accusations against Mr. Fox. Maybe she should take the tag with her too. That way she would have physical proof as well as the photographs.

Vanessa put her hand into the bloody mess and grabbed hold of the tag, pulling it hard. It was still firmly attached to a large piece of whale. Since she couldn't take the whole thing with her, she'd have to find some way of cutting it off.

She looked around quickly, noticing a couple of machetes hanging upside down on hooks close by. Without a second thought, Vanessa grabbed one up. It was heavy and the blood on her hands made it hard to hold, but she sawed at it until it gave way and the tag came off. She stared at her blood-covered hands. It was so disgusting! She was definitely turning vegetarian after all this.

Vanessa put the tag and camera into her backpack and zipped it up. Then she crept along the deck back toward the gangplank. Why had they kept the tag this time? she wondered. Surely that was dangerous for them if they were caught?

No, Vanessa realized suddenly; they were being clever. By leaving the tag on the boat, which moved long distances in the waters where the whales lived, they could fool the scientists in the research center into thinking the whales were alive and swimming around.

Maybe Mr. Fox had told them about Ziggy's tag washing up on the beach. Keeping the tag on board until they were clear of the area would be less suspicious.

The sound of the men's voices grew louder, and Vanessa saw five of them moving in her direction. Crouching behind a pillar, she watched them. It was clear to her that Mr. Fox's friend was the captain. He was barking orders in a language entirely foreign to her.

How was she going to get back onto the pier? Vanessa wondered. She stood for a second and glanced over the side. To her utter astonishment, instead of the harbor, she saw a rocky headland, an empty beach, and a large mountain moving in the distance. Her heart, which was hammering away in her chest, suddenly missed a beat, and Vanessa felt herself getting lightheaded.

They were at sea!

CHAPTER 34

In June 1991 it was reported in the *Victoria Times Colonist* that Terry Osland saw a 30-foot-long animal on a beach in Saanich Inlet. She told the reporter that it slithered quickly into the sea, leaving scrape marks and a foul odor behind it.

Vanessa stared at the moving landscape, desperate to believe that her eyes were tricking her. But the harbor and shops were gone. There were no houses to be seen anywhere. No people or roads. Vanessa wasn't even sure it was still Duquette Island.

How had she missed the motion of the boat? She must have been concentrating too hard on taking photographs and cutting off the tag.

She sank back to the ground, and blind white panic rolled over her in waves like seasickness. What was she going to do?

At first she could hear the whispering but she couldn't understand it. The blood was pumping too loudly in her eardrums and her mind was in freefall. The word began to solidify, circling slowly at first, then getting faster, becoming more insistent.

Jump, Toddy commanded. *Jump, jump, jump, jump!*

Vanessa tried to slow her breathing. She concentrated on the air coming in and out of her nose. That had been one of her mum's tricks when she was stressed about something.

Help me, Mum, Vanessa pleaded silently. Whatever she did, she would have to act quickly. Otherwise she and the boat would be in Alaska before she knew it.

She searched her pockets frantically for her mobile phone and when she couldn't find it, she dived into her backpack. It wasn't there either.

For a second, Vanessa wondered if she should just walk up to the men and admit that she was a stowaway. But what language did they speak, and what would they do to her?

Jump! Jump! Toddy was louder than she'd ever heard him.

Beside her, Vanessa spotted a lifesaving ring. It was the standard-issue sort she was used to seeing in her local swimming pool at home. The cheerful red and white looked out of place on the trawler.

It would be madness to jump, wouldn't it? But which was the better chance of survival: jumping into the water or trusting these butchers to help her?

The sight of yet another empty beach passing by was enough to push Vanessa to make a snap decision. She grabbed the ring and tried to undo the rope. Vanessa was usually good with knots but this was stuck tight by salt and time. She'd need a knife.

Of course, the machete! It was on the deck, not far away.

She ran to get it and, without caring if anyone saw her, she hacked at the rope until it broke. Grabbing up the ring, she threw her bag on her back, climbed the railing, and jumped overboard in a matter of seconds.

Her thumping heart was the only noise she heard.

It was like landing on concrete when she hit the surface of the water. It jarred her whole body, expelling every ounce of air from her lungs, so that when she came back up to the surface she couldn't breathe for many seconds. She clung to the ring for dear life. She half-expected to hear shouts from the deck above but she heard nothing. There were no cries of surprise, no fingers pointing at her. The boat continued on. The wake rocked Vanessa violently for a few seconds, and then it was all over. Within another minute, the boat had rounded a headland and was out of sight. A lone seagull sitting on the surface of the cold gray water was her only companion now.

CHAPTER 35

There are over three hundred claimed sightings of *Cadborosaurus willsi*.

At first Vanessa just drifted, hoping she would be pushed by the current onto the beach. But she was getting cold very quickly and she soon realized that she would have to try and swim with the ring if she was going to make it. She was too tired to cry, too numb to feel anything but the dead weight of her body.

Nobody knew where she was. They wouldn't miss her until dinnertime anyway. By then it would be too late—unless she could make it to the beach.

Suddenly she felt something brush up against her, sending a jolt of electricity through her body. There was something beneath her in the water. The thought terrified her, and she kicked out with every bit of strength she had left. She had to get to that beach.

Until that moment she hadn't even thought about what might be in the water with her. A humpback would be OK, as they only ate plankton, but a killer whale might mistake her for a seal. And what about Caddy? What did it eat?

The creature rose out of the water just in front of her, as though commanded by her thoughts. Vanessa froze, too terrified to swim. She clutched the red-and-white lifesaving ring and prayed feverishly that the beast wouldn't notice her.

But the large ugly head pivoted on its long neck. Its eyes bulged; its jaw dropped open; and then the snakelike coils appeared—huge, heavy, and powerful.

Oh, God! Please help me, Mum, Vanessa pleaded silently. *Make it disappear.*

She watched it sink slowly down into the water

again. But that didn't help. It was bad enough seeing a sea serpent above the water, but how much worse to imagine it swimming beneath her at that very moment!

She felt a current of water rush past her legs and saw it well up around her in a smooth, circular pattern. Vanessa gave a strangled cry, let go of the ring, and swam for her life. The cold had crept into her bones and her teeth rattled in her head like boiled sweets in a jar. With each stroke she got a little weaker.

The beach wasn't all that far. Surely she could make it! Although her clothes and backpack made swimming almost impossible, Vanessa kept kicking. Her lungs were fit to burst when she felt a searing pain in her knee and realized that she was swimming over rocks in the shallows.

She put her feet down, stumbled forward the next few yards, and then collapsed onto her knees. But the sound of a huge splash behind her propelled her forward on all fours like a crab, and she scuttled frantically up the stony beach. She had to get away, find somewhere safe, before she passed out.

Vanessa didn't get very far. Her weight became too much for her arms and she collapsed onto her stomach, exhausted. Her eyelids, the last things to move, came down like shutters.

"Mum!" Vanessa cried out again, but the word never reached her lips. She was slipping away. She had gone too far this time.

CHAPTER 36

Ask many Victoria residents today about Caddy and you will get a blank look. But the reality of the sightings cannot be denied. Over the years too many knowledgeable and observant people have seen a creature unlike any other. Caddy will likely remain in our consciousness, and sightings will occur. But he remains a challenge.

—Stephan Ruttan, Local History Librarian,
Greater Victoria Public Library, May 2009

Vanessa came to and passed out repeatedly over the next few hours. Her head, pressed against the rocks, throbbed, and her body shook violently. Every bit of her was in pain. As dusk fell, her mind unhitched from the physical reality of the place, wove in and out of dark recesses, memories replaced by hallucinations, peopled by monsters. Mr. Fox's lean face transformed into Caddy's huge horselike one, his body stretched to become that of a snake that wrapped itself so tightly around Vanessa that she struggled for every breath. The voices she heard, men's voices, came and went, loud and accusing.

By the time an old-fashioned wooden fishing boat arrived at the island, Vanessa looked like a small bundle of wet rags washed up on the beach. Her pulse was thready and her breathing so shallow that her chest moved imperceptibly.

She came to briefly when she felt hands pulling at her. Through her lashes she saw the face of a man looming over her. Had Mr. Fox come to get her? Terror flared in her eyes, but even in her weakened state she registered that it wasn't Mr. Fox and felt a rush of relief. It was a face she recognized, but she didn't know whose.

Vanessa tried to move her lips, but when she felt herself being lifted gently and heard Lee's soothing voice whispering in her ear, she finally let go. She was safe now. She felt herself falling deep beneath the surface into a peaceful place.

Lee wrapped her jacket around Vanessa and talked softly to her as Tom Tankard carried Vanessa to the boat. Although Vanessa had stirred at first, she appeared totally unconscious now and couldn't be roused.

Lee was on autopilot. They had to get Vanessa back to the guesthouse and get her warmed up as quickly as possible. Lee continued to talk to Vanessa and stroked her head, did all the practical things she was supposed to do, but all the time her heart was breaking.

Lee hadn't been able to find Mr. Fox when the call had come through from Dr. Mitchell. This time the signal hadn't been lost, but had just stopped moving, he told her. It was highly suspicious that it was stationary on a beach. With a sinking heart, Lee knew that she would go and find just the tag again, but she couldn't rest until she was sure. In the end the only person she could find with a boat had been a very reluctant Tom Tankard.

Vanessa now lay along the bottom of the boat,

and Lee cradled her head. Dear God, it was like a rerun of Loch Ness. Only worse. This time Vanessa's dad wasn't even with them. Lee kissed Vanessa's forehead, willing her to stir. Lee steadied herself with the thought that at least Vanessa was alive and didn't seem hurt and that was all that mattered for the moment.

As they pulled up to the beach and Mrs. Bouche and Wayne came hurrying down to the water's edge, Lee bit back her irritation at the sound of Wayne's loud voice.

"What happened to her? Is she dead?"

His voice seemed to be enough to penetrate Vanessa's consciousness. She stirred and moaned.

"What's wrong with her?" Wayne persisted.

"Stop it, Wayne!" Lee said shortly.

When Lee looked down at Vanessa, she felt a wave of relief flood to her very fingertips. Vanessa was smiling! It was a small and feeble one, but it was a smile all the same.

CHAPTER 37

On 21 July 1943 Mr. and Mrs. Spenser and their friend Mrs. Fisher saw Caddy in the water at Grantham's Landing. They said that it had a head like a python, had five or six coils, and was 30 to 40 feet long.

Vanessa slept heavily through the night and into the afternoon of the next day. She woke very slowly, drifting in and out of sleep, aware of the people around her sometimes and gripped by the writhing coils of the serpent at others. Her relief, when she finally came around, at finding herself in bed wearing her familiar white nightdress was so intense that she broke down and sobbed.

"Vanessa, Vanessa, it's OK," Lee said, coming through the bedroom door as if she had been shot from a cannon. She threw her arms around Vanessa and hugged her hard.

"Everything is OK now, you're safe. The doctor says you're fine, really. You just need rest." Lee held her at arm's length and looked into her eyes. "As soon as you're better, we're getting off this island and going home. I promise."

"No, no," Vanessa wailed through her sobs. "The whale. It was all cut up on the boat. In a fridge thing. It was horrible, Lee. The blood was all over me." She grabbed hold of Lee's hands, scratching her with a nail without even noticing.

"It's Mr. Fox, Lee. He's one of the whale hunters," she said ferociously. "You have to find him."

It took Lee a considerable amount of time to calm Vanessa down. She sat on the side of the bed and stroked her hair, deeply worried. What on earth had happened to Vanessa? Why had she been on that deserted island at all?

But Lee decided that she wouldn't ask any questions. She would let it come from Vanessa in her own time.

It didn't take long for the whole story to come tumbling out, and Lee was appalled: the crab boat, the cut-up whale with the tag attached, Vanessa jumping overboard.

Lee put her hands over her eyes and let out a deep groan.

"My God, Vanessa, if you hadn't taken that tag, we would never have found you."

"Taken the tag?" Vanessa echoed looking puzzled. And then her face cleared. "Oh, you mean you tracked me down by GPS like a whale? That was lucky, then."

"I thought I was going to find a tag on the beach, but I found you!" Lee looked pained. "You nearly scared me to death, Vanessa," she added quietly.

"Sorry," Vanessa said meekly. "I only took it so you'd believe me about the whale hunters and Mr. Fox."

"I can't bear to think what might have happened if we . . ." Lee didn't finish her sentence but buried her face in Vanessa's hair and hugged her so hard that Vanessa began to think she might suffocate.

"I'm fine now, though, Lee. Honestly, I'm OK," Vanessa said, pulling away to catch her breath. "You said 'we' just now. Who was with you? I remember a man's face. It wasn't Mr. Fox, though."

"No. It was Tom Tankard," Lee replied.

The answer was so unexpected that Vanessa sat straight up in bed.

"Yes, that's who it was!" she exclaimed. "But how on earth did he get there?"

"Well, I couldn't track Mr. Fox down. Nor could Dr. Mitchell. So I just had to find someone else with a boat."

Vanessa snuggled back down under her covers. "But he hasn't been out on a boat since Ray's accident, they said."

"True. But when I told him about the whales being killed by illegal hunters he was outraged. After that he still took a bit of persuading, but eventually he caved in and agreed to help me. And thank God he did." Lee hesitated, remembering the look on Tom's face on the beach. "He was pretty shocked when we found you. Said you had called to his house one day, but then he clammed up."

"Right," Vanessa agreed noncommittally. She

didn't want to get into that conversation at the moment. "You do believe me about the whales being cut up and Mr. Fox being involved, don't you?" Vanessa asked instead. But before Lee could answer, Vanessa gave a loud gasp and slapped her forehead dramatically. "Oh my God, Lee, I'm being so stupid. My camera, where's my camera?" she demanded. "There are photos of Mr. Fox on the beach with the captain of that crab boat. The one that had the whale on it. If you zoom in you can see Mr. Fox has a GPS tracker in his hand—I'm sure he was selling it. There are pictures of the sliced-up whale too. That would be enough proof for Dr. Mitchell, wouldn't it?"

To Vanessa's surprise, Lee didn't look at all excited. Instead she turned her head a fraction, avoiding Vanessa's eyes.

"What is it, Lee?"

"Your camera was in your backpack, Vanessa. I'm sorry, but the salt water will have destroyed it. There was a book too, and it was ruined."

Vanessa collapsed back onto her pillows and closed her eyes, too disappointed to speak. Her camera, and Jack's last copy of the book about Caddy, destroyed! She felt sick to her stomach.

CHAPTER 38

The presence of strong jaws and sharp teeth suggest a carnivorous lifestyle. There is much debate as to whether Caddy is more likely to be a reptile or a mammal.

Later in the afternoon, Vanessa got dressed. Although she had almost recovered physically from her adventure, she felt very depressed. She lay on her bed and stared at the flaking paint on the ceiling. She didn't want to talk to anyone, not Frankie and certainly not Wayne.

At about four o'clock in the afternoon, Lee came into Vanessa's bedroom to tell her that Tom Tankard and Professor Noire had come by to see how she was.

"Tom and Jack together? That's surprising!" Vanessa said, sitting up and looking interested.

Then she remembered the horrible task ahead of her—she had to tell Jack about his book. She felt so bad. It was out of print now, and that had been his only copy!

"I'll be down in a moment," she said to Lee.

Vanessa dragged herself reluctantly down the stairs.

When she opened the door into the sitting room, she was surprised to see Tom chatting away to Lee. He looked more relaxed than she'd ever seen him.

Jack greeted Vanessa warmly. "Glad to see you're still in one piece," he said with a grin.

"Just about. Thought I was Caddy food there for a while," she said to him under her breath.

Jack's eyebrows shot up.

"I've only heard a little bit of the story from Tom. Obviously there is much more."

"Yes," Vanessa replied. "And I've something awful to tell you."

Jack's kind eyes watched her.

"I had your book in my bag when I jumped over the side of the trawler," Vanessa explained.

"Jumped over the side of the trawler?" Jack repeated, shocked.

"Yes," Vanessa continued, "and now the book is ruined."

There was only a couple of seconds' pause before Jack threw back his head and started to laugh.

Vanessa looked at him in surprise, as did everybody else in the room.

"What?" Vanessa asked, slightly hurt by his reaction.

"What's so funny?"

"You are," he replied, still chuckling. "You're a born cryptozoologist—mad as a March hare. Why would I be bothered about a book when you almost died, Vanessa?"

Vanessa grinned. "I suppose. Thanks," she said simply.

She glanced over at Lee and Tom, who were talking earnestly again.

"I heard you came with Tom," Vanessa said lightly to Jack. "I didn't know you two were pals."

"We're not," said Jack. "I saw Tom walking on the road and I offered him a lift—a neighborly gesture which he typically refuses. Except this time he accepted. Imagine my surprise!" Jack looked amused. "Anyway, I got an even bigger surprise when Tom told me about finding you half-dead on an island, Vanessa, and said that he was on his way to visit you. Naturally, I couldn't resist calling in to see you, although I won't stay long. You look like you need to rest," he added with concern in his eyes.

"I'm fine, physically. It's the damage to your book and my camera that's really bothering me," Vanessa moaned.

"Oh, forget the book," Jack said breezily, "and tell me about your camera."

"It has some photos I really need. They prove that the whales are being hunted by those fishermen and that Mr. Fox is involved too." Vanessa let out a long sigh. "But the camera got wet and the photos are destroyed. Apart from the tag, they were the only evidence I had."

Jack suppressed a smile. "Wow! Cut-up whales, illegal hunters, jumping ship—that's some adventure. But just so you know, Vanessa," he said casually,

206

"although the camera may be damaged, the memory card will be OK. It's like an airplane's black box; it's pretty indestructible."

Vanessa blinked a couple of times, trying to make sense of his words.

"You mean . . ." Vanessa's flow was interrupted by Mrs. Bouche wheeling in a rattling trolley filled with teacups and plates of scones.

"It will be easier if I show you," Jack said to Vanessa.

"Do you really think you can get my photos back?" Vanessa said doubtfully.

"Yes. Do you have a laptop here?" Jack asked.

"Lee, Lee, is your computer in your room?" Vanessa yelled excitedly, knocking into the tea trolley and taking the stairs two at a time without waiting for an answer.

"In my computer bag," Lee shouted after her, looking bewildered. "Sorry, Frankie. She's still a bit excitable after yesterday."

Lee busied herself trying to rescue the few scones which were not now sitting in a pool of tea. She hoped that Vanessa wasn't going to make a scene in front of everyone about Mr. Fox and the photos. It was something she was intending to investigate, but she wanted to do it quietly in case Vanessa had gotten the wrong end of the stick. It wouldn't be the first time.

CHAPTER 39

In February 1954 a group of about thirty people watched Caddy basking on the surface some way from the shore at Nanaimo.

They all stood around the computer while Jack inserted the memory card and brought up the photos. There were lots of pictures—mainly of home, but a few taken on Duquette Island.

"Which one, Vanessa?" said Jack.

"That one," Vanessa said, pointing at a thumbnail, and Jack made it full screen.

They all stared at the picture. It was Mr. Fox and another man on a beach.

"That's the captain of the crab trawler," Vanessa said, pointing him out.

It wasn't exactly incriminating.

"Can you zoom in, Jack? There. See that thing Mr. Fox is holding? It's one of those GPS tracking things. I think he was selling it to the captain that day."

"What was the name of the crab boat, Vanessa?" asked Lee.

"I don't know," Vanessa wailed. "I can't believe I didn't notice and I never thought to ask the girl in Jo-Jo's. She was a bit odd, really. Not sure she would have told me anyway." Vanessa stopped and blushed a little. She was straying off the point and everyone was looking at her.

The sound of the front door banging made them all jump. They could hear Wayne's voice chattering away but not the person he was with.

The door opened and Wayne sauntered in, followed closely by Mr. Fox, who looked mildly surprised but totally unfazed.

"We're just looking at some pictures of you, Eddie," Lee said, cool and unsmiling.

Vanessa was surprised. She had never heard Lee call him anything other than Mr. Fox before.

Mr. Fox looked at the screen.

"Oh, yes," he said casually. "That's the captain of the *Mayflower*. I've known him for decades. It's not often that our paths cross, though. Last time was in Hawaii, when we were both in the tuna fishing business."

It's like trying to catch a squid with your bare hands, Vanessa thought, *slippery and slimy*.

"We've got proof," Vanessa said, tapping the screen with her finger. "You're selling him one of the whale trackers that you stole from Brighton Island."

"Whoa there, little missy. That's quite an accusation, you know." Mr. Fox peered at the screen, angling his head this way and that. "Difficult to make out, really. Most spies use better cameras."

Vanessa felt her face flame red hot. He was so arrogant!

"Well, what about these other photos?" she continued, indicating to Jack to pull up the pictures of the cut-up meat on the trawler.

"Where were these taken?" Mr. Fox arched his eyebrows.

"On the *Mayflower*," Vanessa replied tartly. "Look at those photos. Cut-up whale meat on a crab boat?"

"Did Captain Gudmunsson invite you on, or were you just snooping around on your own?" Mr. Fox smiled at Vanessa as if it was all a big joke.

"How do you explain the whale meat, Mr. Fox?" Vanessa persisted.

"Well, I'm not sure I'd know anything about Mr. Gudmunsson's catch. Could be tuna, don't you think?"

"Perhaps a cetacean expert we both know on Brighton Island could tell the difference between tuna and whale meat," Lee said quietly.

"Of course it's whale meat," said Vanessa. "I found one of the Greenpeace whale-tracking tags embedded in it."

Mr. Fox gave Lee and Vanessa a sullen look.

"What's 'cetacean' mean?" Wayne piped up.

"Marine mammals, Wayne, like whales and dolphins," Lee explained.

Mr. Fox said nothing.

"We could match the GPS position logs of the trawler with the information from the tag that Vanessa found on board," Lee continued to Mr. Fox. "That would prove the tagged whale had been on the boat."

Mr. Fox was beginning to look worried but forced a smile.

"She's just a kid. Who's to say she was ever on the crab boat? Those photos could be from anywhere."

With that he turned and walked out the door, banging it hard.

There was a moment's silence, which Lee broke with a clap of her hands.

"Well done, you!" she said to Vanessa, crossing the room to put an arm around her shoulder. "I'm going to take you right now to Brighton Island so that you can tell Dr. Mitchell the news yourself and he can file an official report."

Vanessa's face lit up. "To the police?"

"To the Department of Fisheries and Oceans," Lee replied. "To be honest, I can't see the police being interested, Vanessa, but there is always the possibility that the DFO could revoke these people's fishing licenses."

"A possibility?" said Vanessa wildly. "A possibility of their licenses being revoked? Is that all, Lee? You mean they won't go to jail for this?"

"No, Vanessa, I'm afraid not. The best we can hope for is that we've brought it to light and that all the conservation groups will make a fuss. But it's not considered a criminal act. The only people who have ever been jailed or arrested have been the antiwhaling groups that are trying to prevent it."

"But that's so unfair. It's wrong."

Lee squeezed Vanessa's hand.

"Yes," she said. "I know, and that's why it's important that people learn the truth. Like you, most people would be on the side of the whales."

Vanessa stared at her blankly.

"And, look, Vanessa," Lee went on, "at least we have unmasked Eddie Fox. He'll certainly never work for Greenpeace again."

Vanessa sighed.

"How will we get to Brighton to talk to Dr. Mitchell?" she asked.

"I'll take you," Tom offered immediately, "seeing as the fox has gone to ground," he added with a chuckle. It was the first time that Vanessa had seen him smile. She gave him a smile back, but it was a very small one.

"Can I come too, please?" Wayne said with a simpering look.

"Not today, Wayne," Lee said firmly. "Vanessa

and I need to talk and then we have to pack. We leave tomorrow. I'm getting her home in one piece if it kills me."

CHAPTER 40

On average there are four to six sightings of Caddy reported a year. They are more frequent in the warmer months—particularly July and August.

The day of their departure threatened to be a stormy one, and there was some concern over whether the ferry would be running or not. Vanessa wasn't worried. She would have loved to stay another couple of days and talk more to Jack about Caddy. But Lee's work was finished for now, and they'd done all they could about the illegal whalers. Dr. Mitchell had been pleased with their report.

And at least Vanessa was going to see the professor one last time before she left. He had rung earlier to offer them a lift. Now everybody was in the kitchen waiting for Jack to arrive.

Vanessa clutched a large white envelope in her hand. It contained her eyewitness accounts of Caddy, describing the creature in as much detail as possible. She had to admit that the first time she had seen it off the boat had been really exciting. But the second time, when she was in the water with the creature, had been absolutely terrifying. Recalling it now brought the hairs up on the back of her neck.

Vanessa looked around. Frankie had gone upstairs, but Wayne's eyes were locked firmly on the envelope she was holding. Then she saw him look over at Lee, who was pulling her purse from her bag.

Vanessa knew that Greenpeace would be paying for Lee's stay at the guesthouse, but it was Lee who would be paying for Vanessa's room. She must remember to thank her properly when they were on the ferry.

"Here's fifty dollars, Wayne, to get your bike repaired," Lee said, handing him the money with a smile.

Wayne looked pleasantly surprised.

Vanessa stared at Lee, stricken. Why had Lee done that? Did she not understand that Wayne had done the damage himself? Vanessa couldn't just sit there and say nothing.

"I didn't burst his stupid tires, Lee," she said angrily. "Why don't you believe me? He did it himself. He was in cahoots with Mr. Fox. He's probably been paid off already."

"Cahoots?" said Lee.

"Yes. All this pestering—"

"That's enough, Vanessa," said Lee. "We'll discuss this later. But meanwhile, Wayne's bike does need to be fixed." Vanessa rolled her eyes. She knew she was right about Wayne.

It was partly affection for Mrs. Bouche that made Lee want to smooth things over before they left. Besides, she would have to return to the island eventually to continue her work and would need a place to stay. It was just as well that Frankie hadn't been there to hear Vanessa's accusations.

Wayne took the money with a cheeky grin.

"Thanks, Lee," he said. "You're the best."

Vanessa turned away in disgust. Wayne was

unbelievable. Really, the sooner Jack arrived and took them out of here, the better.

Wayne stood up, shoved the money into his jeans pocket, and walked out of the room.

Vanessa gritted her teeth.

"He's a horrible liar with not a single redeeming feature," she said angrily. "He's been deliberately making things hard for me, Lee, ever since we got here. Obviously, he's been trying to get rid of me—which means getting rid of you too. Which is exactly what Fox wanted. That's what I meant about being in cahoots."

"You don't think Wayne knew all along about the whales being killed, Vanessa, do you?" Lee looked shocked.

Vanessa shook her head. "No. I don't think he did. But Mr. Fox did use him. He could see that Wayne likes to cause trouble and that he's greedy too. Wayne enjoyed playing along, but that's all, I think."

At that moment, Frankie came back into the kitchen. Vanessa's scowl deepened at the sight of Wayne coming behind her. He was holding something in his hand.

When he held it out to her, Vanessa recognized it immediately.

"What's that?" Lee said, leaning over and trying to make sense of the crude pencil sketch.

Vanessa took the page in silence and was saved from further explanation by Mrs. Bouche.

"Oh, that's so sweet of you, Pickles," she exclaimed, throwing her arms around her son.

Lee looked puzzled.

"It's a peace offering," Frankie explained. "A present for Vanessa."

Lee smiled weakly.

"It's Wayne's drawing of the local sea monster we call Caddy. The one that Vanessa went to talk to the professor about."

As Lee was still looking blank, Frankie was forced to continue with her explanation.

"You know, the professor, the one who's writing the book and who lives at the end of Salem's Lane," said Mrs. Bouche. "Jack. Who's coming to—"

The sound of a car horn honking from the drive cut her off.

"That's Jack now, to take us to the ferry," Vanessa said, grabbing up her backpack. "I'll explain everything when we're on the boat, Lee. I promise."

CHAPTER 41

The Basilosaurus (*Basilosaurus cetoides*) belonged to a group of whales that became extinct about 34 million years ago. It grew up to 65 feet in length and was the largest known animal of its day. With sharp teeth and an elongated body, it has been described as the closest a whale ever came to a snake. Its bones were first mistaken for a sea serpent's.

The good-byes didn't take long. In the end, Vanessa was forced to shake Wayne's hand. Lee had told her it would hurt Mrs. Bouche's feelings if she didn't. Vanessa had become very fond of Frankie, and she also pitied her deeply. She had years of Wayne to get through yet.

"Thanks, Frankie," Vanessa said, when the older woman gave her a great big bear hug. "Your cooking was the best." Vanessa knew she had hit the mark when Frankie beamed happily at her and gave her a second hug.

They put their bags in the trunk and Lee got into the passenger seat beside the professor. Dark clouds were gathering on the horizon.

"Do you remember arriving in that storm, Lee?" Vanessa asked. "Doesn't it feel like weeks ago?"

"Years," Lee replied.

The first drops of rain hit the top of Vanessa's head as she stepped out of the car. The three of them chatted as they walked down to the harbor, Jack insisting on carrying both of their bags.

As the ferry pulled in and ropes were thrown from the deck to the pier to tie it up, Vanessa pushed the white envelope into Jack's hand.

"For your files," she said quietly. "It's a record of both times I saw Caddy, in as much detail as I could remember. There is also a very bad drawing," she explained.

Jack stared at her in surprise.

"You never told me that you'd actually seen Caddy," he said.

"I've not only seen Caddy, I've been in the water with it." Vanessa's eyes widened a fraction. "Scary."

Jack looked pleased. "Do I have permission to use these in my book, Vanessa?"

"Of course," she replied.

"Use what?" Lee asked suspiciously, catching the end of the conversation.

"I'll tell you about it on the ferry, Lee."

"Really, Vanessa, you are impossible," Lee said crossly. "Surely there's not something else you haven't told me about."

CHAPTER 42

The coelacanth was a deep-sea fish alive at the time of the dinosaurs. It was thought to be extinct for the last 65 million years but was rediscovered alive in 1938. The megamouth shark was only discovered in 1976. Is Caddy waiting to be discovered too?

Lee and Vanessa stood on the deck and waved to Jack until he was just a tiny speck. The birds swooped overhead, and Vanessa closed her eyes and breathed in deeply.

"You OK, Vanessa?"

"I'm fine, Lee. Just getting in the last of that Duquette fresh air," she said with a sad grin. "I'm sorry to be leaving. You too?"

"Can't wait to get home!" Lee said with a loud snort. "I need a holiday after that. Come on, let's get a seat inside. You've got things to explain."

They turned to go, but Vanessa was stopped in her tracks by the sight of a man farther down the deck.

"Look!" she hissed. "Lee, look. Can you see him?"

He was making his way slowly toward them, his eyes on Vanessa.

"Lee, can you see him?" Vanessa said urgently. "It's Ray!"

"What on earth are you talking about, Vanessa? It's Tom. Of course I can see him."

It only took Vanessa a couple of seconds to register Lee's words and react.

"Only joking," she said with a chuckle, making a quick recovery.

They shook hands with Tom, Vanessa feeling reassured by his warm, rough palm against her own. It was no ghost this time.

"I thought you didn't use the ferry, Tom?" Vanessa said bluntly.

"No, indeed I don't. Not usually. But after going out in my boat with Lee the other day, I decided it's time to get back to fishing, back to normal life. Time to bury the past. So I'm just going to the mainland today to pick up some supplies for my fishing boat." He caught Vanessa's eye and smiled gently. "I'd forgotten how good it feels to stand on deck. It makes me feel close to Ray."

Vanessa and Lee needed to get out of the wind, so they said good-bye to Tom and went and found a seat in the lounge.

"I'll get us a couple of drinks and then you can tell me everything," Lee said, as Vanessa collapsed onto a seat.

Lee returned a few minutes later. She handed Vanessa a can of Coke and opened one for herself.

"How come you haven't told me about this Caddy thing before now?"

"I was going to, Lee, I swear. It's just that you were really busy with the whale hunting and Wayne kept messing things up for me."

She knew that her excuses sounded really pathetic, but they were partly true.

"Well, we have lots of time now," Lee said

determinedly. "A ferry ride all on our own. That's plenty of time for you to tell me the whole story."

Not entirely alone, Toddy muttered from the comfort of Vanessa's backpack. *And telling the whole story may not be the best idea*, he warned.

Vanessa looked thoughtfully at Lee's trusting face and wondered what on earth she would say. Toddy had a point. Just how much should she tell Lee—and where exactly would she start?

ACKNOWLEDGEMENTS

Many thanks to Dr. Paul LeBlond, scientist and cryptozoologist, who welcomed me to his home on one of the beautiful gulf islands in British Columbia and talked to me at length about Caddy and about his book with Dr. Edward L. Bousfield, *Cadborosaurus: Survivor from the Deep*. I am most grateful for all the information and your time.

Thanks also to Jessica Wilson from Greenpeace in Vancouver, and Anne who runs the fantastic whale-watching tours in Panama. Watching the baby humpbacks that day will stay with me for a long time.

Once again I am indebted to my publishers, Elaina and Siobhán at Little Island, for all their work on this book. Thanks also to my dear friends Jenny and Paula for their helpful feedback on the manuscript. And to my family, Ian, Cal, Myles, and Ollie, for being there when I need them most.

REFERENCES AND FURTHER READING

I've tried to be as factual as I can about the Cadborosaurus sightings. Most of the information is thanks to my interview with Paul LeBlond and material from his book *Cadborosaurus: Survivor from the Deep*. But the cetacean research center on Brighton Island, the place I call Duquette Island, and all its residents are entirely fictitious. The following are references that I've used and make interesting reading on Caddy and environmental issues.

Books

Loren Coleman and Jerome Clark. *Cryptozoology A to Z: The Encyclopedia of Loch Ness Monsters, Sasquatch, Chupacabras and other Authentic Mysteries of Nature.* Simon and Schuster, 1999.

John Robert Colombo. *The Monster Book of Canadian Monsters.* p. 142–153. Battered Silicon Dispatch, 2004.

Betty Sanders Garner. *Canada's Monsters.* Chapter 10, p. 75–82. Potlach Publications, 1976.

Bernard Heuvelmans. *In the Wake of the Sea-Serpents.* Hill and Wang, 1968.

Paul LeBlond and Edward L. Bousfield. *Cadborosaurus: Survivor from the Deep.* Horsdal and Schubert, 1995.

Howard White. "The Cadborosaurus meets Hubert Evans." *Raincoast Chronicles Six/Ten, Collector's Edition II.* p. 276–278. Harbour Publishing, 1995.

Newspapers and Articles

Jeff Bell. "It's prime time for spotting Cadborosaurus." *Times Colonist*. 6 July 1999.

Patrick Murphy. "Three sightings of mysterious Caddy." *Times Colonist*. 27 July 1996.

Patrick Murphy. "Caddy attracts new fans." *Times Colonist*. 21 July 1998.

Websites

www.greenpeace.com
www.seashepherd.org
www.wcs.org
www.forwhales.org
www.gvpl.ca/interests/local-history/tales-from-the-vault/caddy
www.bcscc.ca/cadborosaurus.htm

ABOUT THE AUTHOR

Dr. Jean Flitcroft started her career as a scriptwriter for medical and scientific films, and later became a travel writer when her obsession with travel won out. It was on these journeys around the world that she started writing books for children. She lives in Dublin, Ireland, with her husband and three sons. Learn more at www.jeanflitcroft.com.